Matt raised the microphone to his lips. He felt a buzz of excitement – it was actually happening!

'Thank you for that round of applause,' said Matt, at which point there was a muffled laugh and the audience started to clap. 'At last,' he said with a laugh in his voice.

FABER & FABER has published children's books since 1929. Some of our very first publications included *Old Possum's Book of Practical Cats* by T. S. Eliot starring the now world-famous Macavity, and *The Iron Man* by Ted Hughes. Our catalogue at the time said that 'it is by reading such books that children learn the difference between the shoddy and the genuine'. We still believe in the power of reading to transform children's lives.

HARRY HILL

Illustrated by **STEVE MAY**

90 YEARS OF EXCELLENCE
FABER & FABER

First published in 2019
by Faber & Faber Limited
Bloomsbury House,
74–77 Great Russell Street,
London WC1B 3DA

Printed in the UK by CPI Group (UK) Ltd, Croydon, CR0 4YY
Typeset by MRules

A CIP record for this book
is available from the British Library

ISBN 978–0–571–34567–0

2 4 6 8 10 9 7 5 3 1

1

Didn't You Used to Be Matt Millz?

'Happy birthday, dear Maaaaaatttttt!

Happy birthday to yooooooooou!'

'Congratulations, Matthew!' said his mum as Matt blew out the candle wedged into the top of a chocolate brownie. It was his thirteenth birthday and he was celebrating it with dinner at Piece-A-Pizza, the pizza restaurant in Anglebrook High Street. His family and friends all cheered wildly.

Then it happened.

'Didn't you used to be Matt Millz?' came a voice from over his shoulder. The voice belonged to a woman who'd been sitting at one of the tables by the window. Matt had been aware that she'd been staring, pointing and muttering about him since they'd sat down. She was now standing over him and jabbing him in the shoulder with her finger. He looked up and refocused his eyes on her face. She was smiling.

'Sorry?' he said, trying to stay upbeat.

'I said to my friend, that looks like that boy who was on the box. The comedian on *The T Factor*, the one that was booted off for being too young. Well, she said it couldn't be. She said he wouldn't be eating in a joint like this. She said by now he'd be living in the lap of luxury, but I'm right, aren't I? It is you. Matt somebody, wasn't it?'

'Er ...' hesitated Matt. Over the last six months he'd had to get used to this line of enquiry, but had never really worked out a satisfactory answer. 'Yes, that's right,' he said with a sigh, just wanting her to leave him and his family and friends alone. 'I'm Matt Millz, the once famous, now forgotten, youngest stand-up comedian in the world,' he added sadly.

The woman was slightly taken aback at Matt's tone. 'Oh,' she spluttered. 'I didn't mean ... I was just gonna ... wish you luck,' she said, backing away, obviously wishing she hadn't approached him in the first place.

'Oh,' said Matt, taken by surprise. 'Thank you ... I ... er ... thanks.' He suddenly felt bad for snapping at her when all she'd meant to do was wish him well.

Matt's manager, twelve-year-old Kitty Hope, put a hand gently on Matt's shoulder. 'Hey, come on ...' she said softly, but they both knew that the lady was right.

There was no getting round the fact that it had been almost six months since Matt had stood on a stage and told a joke to a paying audience – and that had been at the Children in Need benefit that his English teacher Mr Gillingham had organised in the school hall.

The gig had gone well – in fact it had gone better than well, it had been amazing. The weird thing was, he hadn't done any of what he called his 'proper jokes', the act he'd worked up from his brilliant experience on *The T Factor*. He'd pretty much gone onstage with just a list of topics he'd wanted to talk about – about his experiences so far in the comedy game – but somehow as he told it, it came out funny. As the first few bits got laughs he'd become emboldened, and suddenly it had become like surfing. He'd been riding the waves of laughs, never quite knowing what was coming up next, and ever-present was the risk of crashing out and failing.

It had been utterly thrilling. The idea that he could work this way, instead of from a learned list of gags, had been a revelation to him and he'd come off the stage desperate to try it again.

'That was so funny, Matt, and so different to what you've done so far!' Kitty had said, screwing her hands into tight little fists of excitement.

'What time did I go on? How long did I do?' he said, looking at his watch.

'You did over twenty minutes!' she trilled.

'Twenty?' said Matt, astounded; he'd only ever done about ten before. 'Wow, it felt like five – seemed to flash by!'

'For the audience too,' she gushed. 'They'd have happily sat through another twenty. Oh, Matt, this is so exciting!'

'I don't remember half of what I said,' he said, looking at the back of his hand and the scribbled list of topics, now smudged with sweat.

'Don't worry,' said Kitty, waving her smartphone at him. 'I recorded it! I'll email it to you later. There's loads of stuff you can develop further. You've started to discover your *voice*!'

'My voice?' said Matt, raising an eyebrow. 'What are you talking about, Kit? I've always had a voice. It's only clowns that don't speak during their act, isn't it?' He hated clowns.

'Your voice! I mean, you're finding the thing that's unique to you,' she said studiously.

'So what was I doing before then?' said Matt, knitting his eyebrows into a frown.

'Well, don't get me wrong, Matt – you've always been funny,' she continued. 'It's just that before . . . well, I could see the influences on you from some of your comic heroes.'

'Influences?' said Matt. He loved to talk about comedy almost as much as he liked performing it.

'Yes, you were doing a lot of one-liners, silly gags if you like – although they were really funny . . .' she said, at pains not to cause any offence. 'But your style was a little bit similar to . . .'

'Eddie's?' said Matt with a nod of his head.

'Well, yes. Not to say you were copying him, just that you were obviously a fan.'

She was right: the Nigerian-born stand-up Eddie Odillo was Matt's total comic idol, top of his list, no contest. Not only did he deliver great gags, he also had what other comics called 'funny bones' – in other words he was physically funny without even having to say a word. Matt's friend, the old variety comic Bobby Bath, said it was the sort of thing you couldn't learn and that you had to be born with – you just had it in you, like some people were born with big feet or blond hair.

Eddie Odillo had told Matt that the only way a comedian could get really good was to practise, to go anywhere, any time for the chance of a gig.

That had been at the heart of his problems since. He just couldn't get any stage time.

No, as he sat surrounded by his friends and family in a pizza joint in the tiny town of Anglebrook, looking at the smoke rising from the candle on his thirteenth-birthday brownie, the reality of his situation seemed suddenly stark. Just like that candle, his comedy career had been blown out – gone in a puff of smoke.

2

A Plan Emerges

'What's the plan then, Kitty?' said Matt's best friend Rob Brown as they were walking back to the car. 'You're supposed to be Matt's agent. Where can he go from here?'

'I've tried everywhere – well, everywhere around here,' Kitty said, gesturing vaguely with her hand. 'There are just no gigs to be had. I did have one thought though . . .' she said slowly.

'Yeah?' said Matt, turning to her, hanging on her every word, like he'd been suddenly woken up from a long sleep.

'Well, didn't you say Ron Wardle at the Comedy

Store had given you his number and told you to call him if you ever needed any help?'

'Yes, yes he did!' Matt's mind flipped back to the night in London when he'd slipped down the road to the world-famous Comedy Store, how he'd stood at the back watching the professional comics at work when Ron, who ran the Store, had approached him with some advice, and was followed closely by Eddie Odillo himself. 'You're right!'

'Well,' said Kitty, raising one eyebrow, 'I think the time has come to take him up on his offer!'

Matt couldn't wait to get home, to follow up on Kitty's idea. He headed straight to his bedroom and flung open his wardrobe door.

'I'm sure I put it in here somewhere,' he mumbled to himself as he rummaged through the pockets of his stage suit. 'Surely I wouldn't have thrown it out …' Then he felt something firm in the lining at the back of the jacket. He put his finger into the nearest pocket. Sure enough there was a hole. He used one hand on the outside of the jacket to slowly inch the piece of card towards the hole in the pocket until he had it between his thumb and forefinger, then he pulled it through the hole and into the light. He flipped the card over and there it was.

London's world-famous
★ COMEDY STORE ★
★ RON WARDLE ★
Manager
Tel: 0207 2684 5873
Email: theboss@londoncomic.co.uk

Matt gave the card a flick then turned to his phone. He took a deep breath and dialled the number.

'Comedy Store, Ron Wardle's office, how can I help?' said a woman's voice on the other end of the line.

'Er, oh . . . is Mr Wardle there please?'

'Who's calling?'

'Oh, um, it's Matt Millz, erm . . . I'm a

comedian . . . I met Ron, I mean Mr Wardle, about six months ago and he told me to—'

'Putting you through, Mr Millz,' said the voice, then there was a click and the line went dead. Matt sighed, assuming he'd been cut off. Well, he figured the Comedy Store must be inundated with comics calling up and trying to get gigs.

Then there was another click and a familiar voice.

'Matt! Long time no see!' It was the slightly nasal tones of Ron Wardle.

'You remember me?' said Matt, more than a little surprised.

'Of course! We don't get that many twelve-year-olds down the Store on a Friday night! How you been keeping? Writing lots of new jokes, I hope. Getting lots of gigs?'

'Er, well . . . yes to the first, no to the second. I'm writing loads of new stuff. In fact I've changed my style quite a lot . . .'

'And you want a gig?' said Ron.

'Er . . . yes . . . yes, if that's possible . . . ?' said Matt.

There was an ominous silence at the other end of the line. 'Uh-oh,' thought Matt. 'I've overstepped the mark here.'

'Yup, that's fine. What are you doing this Friday?' said Ron.

There was a dull clunk as Matt dropped his phone on the carpet of his bedroom floor. He scrabbled down on to his knees to pick it up. 'Hello?!' he said excitedly, putting the phone to his face. 'Hello? Friday? Yes! Yes, I'd love to! Yes! Great . . . I . . .'

'Fine. Don't get too excited. It'll just be an open spot – five minutes – tight, no more, no less, unpaid. You'll be on in the early set after the first interval. Get here for the start if you like and watch the show – otherwise be here no later than eight thirty, please. I'll hand you back to Claudia who will take your contact details. Was there anything else?' said the club manager.

'Um . . . no . . . no, that was . . . I mean, thanks very much, Mr Wardle,' Matt spluttered. 'I won't let you down!'

'Good. See you Friday, Matt.' With that there was a click and Claudia came back on the line.

'You see, he's not the ogre that people make him out to be,' she trilled. 'Mind you, he has his moments.'

'I heard that,' growled Ron's voice in the background.

Matt came off the phone, feeling light-headed. Friday? That was the day after tomorrow!

3

Twenty-Four Hours to Come Up With an Act

'OK, what are you going to open with?' said Kitty, sitting forward in her chair in the DMC (or Disused Mobile Classroom) at first break the next day. Matt hadn't wasted any time: she was the first person he'd called as soon as he'd come off the phone to Ron.

'Well, that's my problem, Kit,' said Matt, running his hand through his floppy fringe. 'Do I do my tried-and-tested act – the gags, the one-liners, the stuff that I know works, or do I have a go at this new "voice" thing you were talking about? The more laid-back, observational version of me?'

'You should really follow your heart on this,' said Kitty. 'That new stuff went down a storm at the school show . . .'

'Yes, but that was to a bunch of kids who know me, not a bunch of strangers in a comedy club. And not just any comedy club – the Comedy Store, for crying out loud. Where I'll be up against seasoned professional comics. What do I do? I've got just over twenty-four hours to come up with an act!'

He was pulling at his hair now, and pacing up and down, something he normally only did before he was due to go on stage.

'OK, take a deep breath and let's just calm down,' said Kitty, shuffling through a selection of Matt's old set lists on the desk in front of her. 'Remember the old rule – always start with your best gag, then we can work back from there. What's your best gag?'

'Well, probably the rusk one? "You're looking at

me thinking he's young – yes, in fact I'm so young if I have a drink I fancy a rusk with it!'"

Kitty grinned and nodded. 'That's a great gag. That will always get laughs and it sets the scene – it acknowledges that you're a kid, and takes the mickey out of yourself too. Good. That's your opener. Then I suggest you go into your new stuff, but keep some of the sure-fire one-liners up your sleeve just in case you get into trouble.'

Matt joined her at the desk as she got a fresh piece of A4 paper and wrote 'Comedy Store' on the top of it with a Sharpie. He could see the sense in what she was saying and the rising panic started to subside.

'Now, what was your favourite bit of the new stuff?' she asked, her pen hovering over the page.

'Well, I guess the stuff about living at home with your parents and them choosing all your clothes and meals?' he said tentatively.

'Ha! Yes! That was great! I loved the line about letting a middle-aged woman choose your

underpants!' she said, letting out an involuntary laugh as she wrote 'Living at home' in big letters under the word 'Rusk'. 'This is a really strong start, Matt,' she said. 'Now, what should we put in next? A quick one-liner?'

'How about the self-service tills routine?' he offered.

'Yeah, great ...' she said with a chortle.

And so it went on until they had a healthy-looking set.

'We just need one last thing. Your closer,' she said.

They both knew that next to the opening gag, his

closing bit was of utmost importance. If the purpose of his opener was to get the audience onside quickly, the feeling they got from his closing gag would be the feeling they associated with him as they left the venue and probably from that day on. It wasn't enough to start well. You could start well, even have a good middle, but a poor ending could kill your chances of a future booking stone dead.

They spent the next twenty minutes looking through Matt's notebooks at some of what he thought were his strongest ideas.

'What's "Medway Rap"?' said Kitty, alighting on one particular heading.

'Oh that. Well, I haven't thought it through properly yet. The idea is, it's a rap about Kent,' said Matt with a smile. 'I've got a few lines like, "Down the M2 and round the bend, before you know it you're in Gravesend. Here's some excitement if you know what I mean, their leisure centre just got a wave machine!" Then it goes on about some other Kent stuff.'

'Ha! That's great!' said Kitty, throwing her head back, genuinely laughing again. 'And it's always good to finish on a song.'

'Yes, I remember Bobby telling me that. He said after a song the audience feel like they have to applaud. It needs a lot of work though,' said Matt, flicking through the rough notes he'd made for the song in his little black book.

'You don't get anything without hard work, Matt. You know that by now,' said Kitty. 'Do you think you can work it up for tomorrow night?'

'I can try,' said Matt.

'Go for it!'

And he did. As soon as he got home from school, Matt started working on the rap and it slowly began to take shape. He had a break for his dinner and then went straight back to it.

Looking at it afresh he could see that it was too long and some bits were stronger than others. Gradually he trimmed it down and honed it before reciting it out loud, timing it with his phone. It was still nearly three minutes. That was far too much of his allotted five-minute set, so he went back and cut anything he felt wasn't a big laugh, then ran it again. It was now coming in at just over a minute. That was still pretty long, but if he cut it down any more it would be so slight as to be hardly worth doing. It was just after ten o'clock at night when he called Kitty and performed the rap for her down the phone.

'It's great, Matt!' she said. He breathed a sigh of relief. 'How long's it running at?'

'Just over a minute,' he said.

'Wow, it seemed less – and it's got a big laugh at the end. Have you learned the rest of your set?'

His heart sank again. 'Not yet, that's my next job.'

'Good, well I'll see you in the DMC at first break tomorrow to run the whole thing, but Matt, you've got a big day tomorrow so try and get some sleep.'

Easier said than done. Sleep was the last thing on his mind now. As he lay in bed Matt kept running his set over and over in his mind, then the rap, and the more he ran it the more confused it became – punchlines became attached to the wrong set-ups, odd words popped up out of nowhere, the whole thing just became an enormous jumble.

When he finally did get to sleep he dreamed the dream he'd been having a lot recently – where he was onstage and he couldn't remember a single line of his act! He'd be onstage at a club or a theatre and there'd be a bright spotlight shining in his eyes, so bright that he could hardly keep his eyes open, and in front of him were the swollen faces of the crowd – expressionless, unsmiling – and all around total silence, the only noise his stuttering attempts to remember his gags. Then when he reached into his inside pocket to sneak a look at his set, he'd unfold the piece of paper to find it completely blank . . .

4
Destiny's Child

It was dark as Matt made his way out of the stark fluorescent lighting of Charing Cross station and on to the cobbled courtyard in front of it. It was cold but it was that crisp sort of cold that clears the head. He knew exactly where he was going – he'd rehearsed the route he'd walk almost as much as his act. Like a homing pigeon, he made his way across the road, then up through Trafalgar Square towards the fourth plinth, which was currently occupied by a huge hand offering a giant thumbs up.

'Let's hope it's a sign ...' muttered Matt as he turned up a narrow lane to the left of the imposing

National Gallery, which in turn led to the road where the Comedy Store was located in a basement below an office block.

As he approached Mark, the huge man-mountain of a bouncer guarding the door, he cleared his throat and looked up. Before he could say anything the bouncer thrust out his hand in greeting.

'Hello, Matt. Long time no see!' he said with a broad grin that showcased three gold teeth. 'I didn't know you were comin' down tonight.'

Matt grinned back; he loved the idea that the doorman at Britain's premier comedy club actually knew his name!

'Hi, Mark,' he said, shaking the man's hand.

'You doing a spot tonight or just watching?' asked Mark, his breath forming little plumes of vapour as it condensed in the cold night air.

'My name should be on the door. Mr Wardle booked me in for an open spot,' said Matt nervously. Saying those words suddenly brought home the reason he was here and what lay in wait. This wasn't like his last visit – this wasn't for fun – this was very much for work!

'I thought so,' smiled Mark. 'The punters are always a bit more relaxed than the acts! Mind you, some of them are so relaxed I'm unable to let them in, if you know what I mean, her-her-her!' he chortled, his shoulders shaking as he laughed at his own joke. 'You remember the way, don't you? Down the stairs and through the double doors,' he said, swinging open the front door.

'Cheers, Mark,' said Matt and stepped forward into the hot mugginess of the club.

'Oh, and Matt . . .' said Mark.

'Yes, Mark?' said Matt, turning back to face him.

'Good luck!' said the bouncer with a huge grin.

Matt nodded and continued on down the steep stairs towards the basement.

As he reached the double doors he could hear music and the sound of people chatting loudly. It took him back to the first and last time he'd been to the club – the night he'd met Ron Wardle *and* bumped into his comedy hero Eddie Odillo again. Now, nearly six months later he was back, not as a spectator this time but as a bona fide performer.

He looked around at the purpose-built club. The layout was tailor-made for comedy – a central stage surrounded by a horseshoe of raked theatre-style seating for four hundred people. *Four hundred!*

Matt took a deep breath. 'Well, I'm here. There's no turning back now . . .' he muttered to himself, then pushed through the crowd towards the dressing-room door.

He was immediately surprised at how tiny and cramped the room was. It was really no wider than a corridor. A youngish man, maybe in his early twenties, was sat studying a piece of paper that Matt assumed was his set list. An older woman sat opposite him under a ropey old TV on a wall bracket, looking at her phone. And a long-haired man in his forties wearing jeans and a waistcoat was pacing the room.

The older woman glanced up from her phone and briefly looked Matt up and down. 'Blimey, they get younger every day,' she said with a sniff, then went back to her phone.

'Do excuse my rude friend,' said the man with the long hair and shook Matt by the hand. 'Her name is Jo Bourke and she's very old, I'm afraid. I'm Mickey and I'm your compere for the night.'

'Yes! I've seen you before!' said Matt enthusiastically. 'I was here about six months ago – in the audience. You were great, the way you handled the hecklers!'

'Hmmm, well that's nice to hear, but you'll have to be a bit more specific. It sounds like every night I've ever done down here!' said Mickey. 'They all merge into one when you've been doing it as long as I have.'

'He's very old,' said the woman, without even looking up from her phone.

'Touché,' said Mickey. 'So look …' he said, changing the subject abruptly and addressing an A4 sheet of paper pinned to a tatty corkboard on the wall above a mini fridge. It was headed 'Running Order'. 'You're the open spot, right? Now what's your name?' He ran his finger down the list.

'Matt!' said Matt. 'Matt—'

But before he could finish Mickey's finger had stopped at his name on the list. 'Oh! Jo! We have a TV star in our midst! This is none other than Matt Millz! The youngest stand-up comic in . . . was it the world or just Britain?' he said sarcastically.

Matt blushed. 'Well, certainly Kent!' he joked.

Mickey laughed. 'The youngest comedian in Kent, yes, I like that! Now you're down for five, and I warn you, Ron's a bit of a stickler about timings, so go over it at your peril! You'll get a red light at four and a half – to tell you to start wrapping it up.'

'Well, that's cool, because I will be rapping it up – I'm finishing on a rap, about Kent,' said Matt brightly.

'Doing less than your full five is fine, but don't take the mick. The sooner we get done, the sooner we all get home as far as I'm concerned!' said Mickey, looking at his watch.

'Amen to that,' said Jo, her gaze still fixed on her phone.

'They enjoy it really,' chirped the other, younger comic who Matt now vaguely recognised. 'Hi, Matt,' he said offering his hand. 'I'm Jeff Crimson.'

'Jeff Crimson!' exclaimed Matt. 'Yes! I've seen you on *Scoff at the Week* – you do really funny stuff . . . although I'm not mad about that show."

'I'm warming to him,' said Jo, who this time looked up at Matt and smiled. 'Load of old rubbish if you ask me. All the gags are scripted but they're pretending to make it up as they go along.'

'Ah, you're just sore they haven't asked you,' said Mickey giving her a playful slap on the back.

'I wouldn't do it even if they did," she said. 'Whatever happened to integrity?'

'I sold mine to the producers of *Scoff at the Week*!' said Jeff with a smirk. 'And I tell you what, you only need to go on that show a few times and doors open for you. Look at Russel Perkins. He went on it twice and now he's selling out the O2!'

'Huh! I heard they hardly sold any tickets for that tour and that idiot at Excalibur had to paper it,' said

Jo. 'I heard Russel lost his shirt on the deal and is up to his eyes in debt.'

'Ignore them, they're old and bitter,' joked Jeff. 'First time at the Store?'

'Yes, yes, as a comic . . .' said Matt.

'I remember my first time down here. Phew! Tough!' Matt's face fell.

Jo turned to him and grinned. 'It is what it is, Matt. If you storm it – great, but if you bomb, it's not the end of the world. There'll be other gigs.'

Just then the door to the dressing room opened and a man's head appeared. He was virtually bald with a thin wisp of blond hair sticking up at the front. 'Five minutes, Mickey! Boss says remember to keep it tight!'

'Thanks, Stan,' said Mickey. Stan nodded and retreated back through the door. 'Right, girls and boys, you heard the man, five minutes! Any further questions, Matt?'

'Yes, where's the toilet?' said Matt meekly.

'Through there.' Mickey pointed at a door at one

end of the dressing room and Matt walked up to it and pushed his way in.

Suddenly he was alone. He looked in the mirror and almost didn't recognise himself. How mad was this? Here he was, just thirteen years old, on his own in the big city, in the loo of none other than the Comedy Store. He used the toilet, then washed his hands and splashed some cold water on to his face to try and help him concentrate. Then he heard a low rumble – it was audience applause.

The show had started!

5

Trouble in Store

It turned out that the TV mounted on the wall of the dressing room offered a view of what was happening onstage, so between running through his set and taking far too many gulps of water, Matt was able to keep an eye on how the show was unfolding.

Mickey had gone out at the top of the show all guns blazing – he'd picked on a couple of people in the front row, making fun of their clothes to establish that he was in charge, then he'd done a couple of topical gags and was now explaining how the night would work.

'If you want to heckle – heckle me!' he said,

standing with his hands on his hips, scowling, half encouraging them to try their luck. 'But please enjoy the acts – they are here to entertain you, and what an act we have to start the show. You may have seen him on TV but try not to let that cloud your judgement! He's actually one of the best new stand-ups around – give it up for Jeff Crimson!'

With that Jeff walked past Matt, through the door at the far end of the dressing room and on to the stage.

'How's it look?' said Jo to Mickey as he wandered back into the dressing room, barely glancing up from her phone.

'Bit Friday night, but they'll be fine once they've settled down,' he said, opening the mini fridge and helping himself to a bottle of water.

'Bit Friday night?' said Matt, always eager to pick up any inside information on the life of the stand-up comic.

'Yeah, it's the last day of the week, most of them will have come straight from work, and they're still a bit wound up, so Friday nights you tend to have to work a little harder. It's "Thank God It's Friday" for them, but less so for us. Saturday nights are much easier because they've had the day to relax, they've spent some time getting ready to go out, there's more of a sense that they're out for fun from the start.'

'Yeah, and Sunday's as dead as a doornail!' chipped in Jo.

'Yeah,' agreed Mickey. 'Sunday they tend to be smilers.'

In what seemed like no time at all Jeff was coming off to a massive round of applause. He stepped back into the dressing room, his face red and sweaty and

his eyes wide with excitement. He took out a hanky and wiped his brow.

'Phew! That was fun! There's a couple of mugs up the back who might be trouble though,' he said taking a mouthful of water from a bottle.

'Just two?' said Jo. 'Makes a change – usually there's about ten of 'em!'

'Anyway, I'd better get going,' said Jeff, grabbing his coat off a peg on the back of the dressing room door. 'I'm closing at the Banana Club.'

'You've got another gig?' said Matt, surprised and more than a bit jealous.

'Yeah,' said Jeff. 'I'm doubling up, then I'm back here to close the late show, right, Mickey?'

Mickey nodded and rubbed his fingers together. 'Nice payday, and the same tomorrow night! All right, let us know if you're running late.'

'Will do,' said the younger comedian stepping out of the dressing room and into the crowd.

'Right,' said Mickey, looking at his watch. 'In approximately fifteen minutes it's your turn, Matt, OK?'

Matt nodded and tried to swallow, but his mouth was as dry as a cream cracker.

He spent most of the interval back and forth to the loo and before he knew it Mickey was gearing up to start the second half.

'Follow me, Matt,' said Mickey, 'and I'll show you the layout backstage.' He pushed open the door at the far end of the dressing room and Matt followed him into the darkness. It was basically a continuation of the narrow dressing room, except it was virtually pitch-black. The only light there came from the flickering LEDs on a huge stack of electrical equipment on the back wall, and the slivers of light that made their way through the cracks in the door in front of them that led to the stage.

'I'll just settle 'em down then bring you on,' said Mickey, straightening himself up and putting his hand to the door. 'Remember, five minutes tops. Look out for the red light at four and a half, which is your signal to start finishing up.' The compere pushed open the door and strode on to the stage.

There was a bit of a cheer, and the audience chatter quickly subsided as Mickey took control.

Matt looked at the wall of electrical equipment behind him. There was a bright yellow sticker with a jagged black shard of a spark printed on it along with the words 'Keep Away! Danger of Death!'.

'Danger of death?' thought Matt. 'Not ideal backstage at a comedy club!'

Then he heard his name being announced by Mickey and another muffled round of applause. Matt pushed the door open and walked the few feet that put him onstage. Mickey patted him on the back as he passed him and leaned in to whisper, 'Break a leg, don't leave any gaps – they'll jump in!'

Matt nodded and walked purposefully towards the mic, grabbed it with both hands and pulled it out of the stand. There were a few murmurs – he was used to that, surprise at how young he was, which fed perfectly into his first line.

'Aaah,' sighed a woman about three rows from the front. 'In't 'e sweet! He's just a kid!'

Without thinking, Matt jumped in. 'Mum?' he said with a pained look on his face. 'Dad said I'd find you here!' There was a big laugh, and Matt pressed the heckle put-down home. 'He says you've got to give up the drink and come home!'

This time it was a massive laugh. Matt laughed too – he'd surprised himself. Riding the laugh, he jumped straight in with his first line. 'Yeah, you noticed I'm younger than most of the acts on the bill. I'm so young, if I have a drink I still fancy a rusk with it!' Another big laugh. He couldn't have hoped for a better start. He'd bought their confidence in his opening ad-lib, and it looked like they now trusted him to deliver. Audiences love an off-the-cuff remark – it makes them feel they are getting a one-off special performance. The only danger with an ad-lib is the rest of your act can look a bit stiff when you go back to it.

'Now's the time to hit them with the new stuff,' he thought to himself and launched into the bit he'd tried at the benefit. 'So who else here has their mum choose all their clothes for them?' Another big laugh, then he had a quick thought. He looked down at a dowdy man in the front row wearing an old jumper and corduroy trousers. 'Apart from you, mate!' he said. Another big laugh.

Then he went into his routine about how his mum bought his underpants for him, which got some big laughs. There were a couple of lulls, but before he knew where he was he could see the red light up at the back behind the audience which told him his time was nearly up.

Nearly up! But he hadn't even started the Medway Rap! He looked across at Stan in the tech booth, who nodded. He was being told to wind up his act and there was loads of stuff he hadn't had a chance to try! Plus he needed to finish on that big laugh. Surely it was better to go a bit over his time if it meant he'd finish on a high? The rap was only a minute long, surely he was allowed a measly minute. He made a snap decision to launch into his final bit.

'Anyone in from Kent?' he cried. From the corner

of his eye he was aware of Stan shaking his head, but having started the routine he had no choice and ploughed on.

'Here we go! Clap your hands!' he shouted and got the crowd clapping along, giving him a beat to rap to. Then off he went:

'I tell you, brother, what you gotta do,
Jump in your car and get down the A2
Medway towns I wanna get at 'em.
Take the A289 road down to Chatham!
Where the ring-road system makes
    driving heaven,
They got a new bus station in 2011!
Take the A226 if you got time to spend
To the Royal Naval Dockyard in Gravesend!
There's something for the kids they'll
    surely be keen.
Coz Splashes in Rainham got a
    wave machine!'

About twenty seconds into the rap the red light started to flash. After forty-five seconds Stan started waving at him. At a minute, fortunately he was done – to a massive cheer and a round of applause that raised the roof.

'I've been Matt Millz!' bellowed Matt above the din. 'That's all from me, goodnight!' Then he turned towards the door at the back of the stage, where Mickey was standing – and he didn't look happy.

'Boss wants to see you,' he hissed as they passed each other.

Matt made his way through the dark backstage area and back to the dressing room. Suddenly all the stress from the last couple of days was gone like a firework exploding. He was buzzing, high on adrenaline. He'd done it! He'd actually played the Comedy Store and killed!

'Enjoy that?' said Jo, smiling for the first time that night.

'Yeah, you bet!' he said, full of energy, unable to wipe the grin off his face.

Just then the door burst open and there was Ron Wardle, with a face like an angry Rottweiler.

'What was that?' he said angrily.

'Huh?' said Matt, caught completely off guard.

'How long were you supposed to do?' snarled the club manager.

'Um . . . about five minutes, Mr Wardle,' said Matt.

'Not *about* five minutes. Five minutes. On the dot. Just five minutes. Do you know how long you did?'

'Well, I mean, I know it was a bit over but . . .' spluttered Matt.

'Seven minutes,' snapped Ron. 'If everyone did as long as they liked, what do you think would happen?'

'Um . . . I don't know . . . I mean, I hadn't got to my closing bit and the five minutes . . .'

'If the five minutes is up and you haven't got to your precious closer then you get off, or better still, you make sure you have got to your closer!' he said, shaking his head.

'Oh, give him a break, you old grouch!' chimed in Jo. 'So he did a couple more minutes than he should.

He stormed it! Give the crowd a shorter interval.'

'The interval's when I make my money,' Ron snapped back. 'On the bar takings! If everyone ran over by two minutes—'

'The show would be eight minutes longer, you tight-fisted old fool!' said Jo.

Ron hesitated, then his face broke out into a broad grin. 'Ha! Fair point, but you know the rules, everyone knows the rules and I won't have it in my club, all right?'

'Yes, sir, sorry, Mr Wardle. Won't happen again,' said Matt. Suddenly the thrill of the gig had given way to bitter disappointment, knowing he'd upset the very person he had been out to impress.

'No it won't,' said Mr Wardle, but his harsh attitude was softening. There was a beat or two as Matt stared at his shoes and Ron tried to look busy.

'I suppose you want to know what I thought of the act?' said Ron, breaking the awkward silence.

'I think you've told me that,' whispered Matt dolefully.

'Well …' began Ron. 'Apart from the timing issue … Jo's right. It was great!'

'Eh?' said Matt, hardly believing his ears.

'You're talented. I'd like to have you back.'

'Yeah?' Suddenly Matt was back up again.

'Yes. I mean, you're not ready for a full booking yet – you need some practice. But give Claudia a call on Monday and I'll book you in for another open spot in six months' time – it'll give you a chance to get some more stage time under your belt. How's that?'

'Another open spot?' said Matt.

'Yes, in six months. Give me a call on Monday.' With that Ron turned and headed back out into the club.

Matt stood there stunned for a moment. It was great that Ron wanted him back, particularly after he'd outstayed his welcome, but six months? That was a lifetime away!

And it wasn't as if he was likely to get any stage time between now and then anyway.

'It's good news,' said Jo. 'Believe me, Ron's tough. Most of the time he gives 'em a year before bringing them back. Take it from me, another five in six months, that means he likes you – even though you ate into his precious bar takings. You should be proud of yourself.'

'I guess I am . . .' said Matt. 'It's just that everything seems to move so slowly.'

Maths wasn't his strong point, but by his calculations, allowing six months between each five-minute open spot, it would take him two and a half years to come up with a solid twenty-minute act. Two and a half years!

He sank into a despondency bordering on despair.

6
Throwing a Sickie

When Monday morning came round Matt felt so down in the dumps he decided he really couldn't face going to school, so when his mum came in to wake him he told her he had a sore throat and a temperature.

'You don't feel especially hot,' she said, sitting on the edge of his bed and putting her hand on his forehead. 'You're probably worn out from the late night on Friday. Perhaps you'd be better off at home today. Ian and I will both be out, but if you're OK in the house on your own . . .'

Matt groaned and nodded.

So that's what he did; he stayed in bed. Well, after his mum and Ian had left for work he got up for a couple of hours to watch TV, then made himself some lunch, but for the rest of the day he just lazed around in bed.

The next morning when his mum came to check on him, he did the same. He just didn't feel like going to school or doing anything if he couldn't do what he loved – stand-up comedy.

'What's the point?' he thought. 'I'm not going to learn anything that's going to help me do what I want to do in life. How does learning about the forces of gravity or the Battle of Hastings help me become a stand-up?'

But the fact was, he wasn't sitting at home writing jokes or rehearsing his act either.

The same thing happened the next day, and then on Thursday morning there was a knock at his door.

'Come in,' he croaked, feigning an advanced case of laryngitis. His mum popped her head round the door.

'The doctor's here to see you,' she said before

darting back out. In walked a man in a white coat with a shock of jet-black hair and a stethoscope round his neck.

'*Gooden morgen*,' he barked. 'I am Doctor Sasparilla,' he said in a thick German accent. He had rather pronounced teeth which interfered with the way he talked to the extent that every time he said a word with an 'S' in it, he showered Matt with saliva. 'I am here to examine you! Now open your mouth and say, "Ah!"'

Matt did as he was told. 'Aaaaah!' he said.

'No, longer, like so – AAAAAAAAAAAAAAA-AAAH!' said the doctor. In addition to the free shower, every time the doctor moved his head Matt got covered in huge amounts of what could only be dandruff.

'Aaaaaaaaaaaah!' sang Matt.

'No! Too long that time!' snapped Doctor Sasparilla, jerking his head to the right and giving Matt another dousing of dandruff.

'Aaaaah!' crooned Matt.

'Good. With a voice like that you're through to boot camp! Now I want you to stand by the window please,' he said, snapping open the curtains.

Matt reluctantly stood up in his pyjamas, walked over to the window, opened the curtains and stared out.

'Right, I want you to stick your tongue out pleeeeease,' said the doctor.

'Erm, why's that, Doctor?' said Matt, a little confused. He'd seen a doctor before and he'd never been asked to do that!

'Well, I don't like the people who live opposite!' said the doctor, only this time he appeared to be stifling a laugh. 'Now I need to take some blood – I find ze eye is ze best place,' he said, producing a huge syringe from an old-fashioned leather bag.

It was then that the penny dropped – Matt suddenly recognised the man in the white coat. It was his old friend, veteran comic Bobby Bath!

'Bobby?' he said.

'Ah! Ha ha! I wondered how long it would take you!' said the doctor, pulling off his wig. 'I thought you'd suss me out with the tongue gag!' he chuckled. 'That's one of Tommy's – Tommy Cooper's. I saw him do it, summer season in Weston-super-Mare. Priceless, always brought the house down!'

'I thought you'd gone on a cruise,' said Matt.

The last time he had seen his friend had been the night before the school benefit gig, when Matt had been due to perform at the Apollo but had pulled out at the last minute – allowing eighty-two-year-old Bobby Bath to take his place. Matt remembered how

Bobby had stormed the gig, but then collapsed in the wings as he came off with a major heart attack. After hospital, he'd gone on a long holiday to recuperate.

'Yes, I did, but now I'm back – and I've got more gigs booked in for this next six months than I've had for the last twenty years!' said Bobby, taking a seat on the end of Matt's bed. 'Phew! I'm tired though. A word of advice, don't have a heart attack! Now what's all this I hear about you staying in bed for days on end?' he said, suddenly getting uncharacteristically serious.

'I'm fed up, Bobby,' said Matt, flinging himself back on to the bed melodramatically. 'Your career may be on the up but mine's stone dead.'

He then explained to Bobby about how he'd had no proper gigs since the school benefit night, how he felt he was on the brink of developing a new style but had a huge wait for a return open spot at the Comedy Store.

'Look,' said the older comic, 'it's corny, I know, but that's showbiz. Nothing necessarily goes the way you want, when you want it. There's no answers except don't give up!'

'That's what Eddie Odillo told me before,' said Matt.

'There you are then,' said Bobby. 'All I know is if you give up completely and lie around in bed all day the chances of you getting anywhere are zero. Besides, what are you going to write jokes about? The size and shape of your pillow? No. You need to get up, son, and get back on the horse.'

'That's just it,' said Matt. 'There is no horse. The horse galloped off six months ago and no one's seen it since!'

'Yeah, well maybe you need to get a new horse!'

7
Business as Usual

And that's how it was. Matt went back to school and knuckled down to lessons. The months went by, and he still wrote gags in his little black book, but the idea of actually becoming a stand-up comic started to fade.

He let go of the idea much as you might get over a broken friendship or the loss of a favourite pet. He moved on, got his head down and concentrated on his schoolwork. He had exams to work towards now, and there'd been a sharp increase in the amount of homework they'd been getting too.

He and his friends were also all pursuing their own interests: Rob had thrown himself into his art and graphics course; Ahmed was really into his tech stuff and was developing computer apps; Neil Trottman – body-popping poet and rapper, also on Kitty's books – was into his music, passing around MP3s of his raps, and even had his own YouTube Channel. Magda Avery had a part-time job helping her mum in the salon at weekends, and even Kitty had become pretty elusive.

She'd always been a bit of a bookworm, but now she too had thrown herself into her schoolwork and spent most of her time in the library – which wasn't really on Matt's radar. Whenever he did see her she assured him she was still working on getting him some more gigs, but it was kind of unspoken between them that they both knew it was pretty unlikely.

The fact was, the odds of becoming a working stand-up comedian were stacked against a teenage boy in rural Kent.

One morning, however, as Matt ambled over to the science block for his first lesson of the day, he caught sight of someone he thought he knew. She was standing with her back to him but he was sure he recognised that dark hair and willowy outline.

'Alex?' said Matt, approaching her and tapping her on the shoulder. As she turned to face him his hunch was confirmed. It *was* Alex – the girl with a real talent for impressions he had met last year at the Frittledean gig. Save for the occasional group chat, he'd all but lost touch with her.

'Matt,' said Alex with a big smile. 'Boy, am I glad to see you!'

'Hang on,' he said a little confused. 'I know you're an impressionist and that's a great impression of an Anglebrook schoolgirl, but what are you doing here? You're at posh, private St Winifred's, aren't you? Don't tell me you got expelled!'

'Not expelled, no ...' said Alex, her eyes suddenly filling with tears. 'My mum and dad split up about three months ago, so basically there's money stuff going on and they can't afford the fees any more. So I'm here!'

'Wow! That's harsh!' said Matt.

'Yeah, just a bit,' she said with a sniff but putting on a brave face. 'I hate new schools ... but at least I know a few people here – you, Kitty, Neil ...'

'Exactly,' said Matt reassuringly. 'You'll fit right in, no probs.' It was really good to see her. 'How's your act coming along?' he asked as he took her over to meet Rob and Ahmed. 'Done any more gigs?'

She shook her head. 'Not since the last time I saw you – at the benefit night. It's a shame because I felt like I was beginning to get the hang of it a bit.'

'I'm the same,' said Matt. 'It's just rubbish round here for gigs. I did start writing a lot of stuff but without a chance to try it out what's the point?'

'Head wants to see you urgently!' said Mr Gillingham, interrupting their reunion.

'Urgently?' said Matt with a frown.

'Yes, so I suggest you get your skates on and trot over there right now!'

'What's it about, sir?' said Matt, doing up the top button of his shirt and adjusting his tie – Mr Pavey was a stickler for correct school uniform.

'Look, Matt,' said Mr G, a little more sternly. 'I'm not his messenger boy – it's bad enough that I've had to interrupt my lunch break to come and find you, so don't push it! But I would have thought the best way to find out what Mr Pavey wants is to go and see him!'

'Yes, sir,' said Matt and headed off towards the main building.

'Ah, Matthew, come in!' said Mr Pavey from behind his desk as Matt was shown into his office. 'Please sit down.'

Matt sunk down in the chair opposite the head.

'I'll get straight to the point,' said Mr P. 'I'm a little concerned about your career!'

Matt squirmed slightly in his chair. It was true he hadn't been doing as well as he might have in his schoolwork, particularly maths and physics.

'Yes, sir, well I'm intending to spend a lot more time on my physics and Miss Stake – I mean, Miss Stark – has suggested I take extra maths . . .'

'No no no,' said Mr Pavey, waving his hand

dismissively. 'Not your *school*work! Your career in entertainment!'

'Oh,' said Matt, more than a little confused.

'How long has it been since you had a gig?' said Mr Pavey, narrowing his eyes.

'Hmm, a while, probably six months ...' In fact, he knew exactly how long it had been – five months and twenty-four days.

'Six months!' repeated Mr Pavey, shaking his head in despair. 'And it's even longer since you were on television or had a story written about you in a national paper.'

'Yes, well that too. One feeds on the other, sir. If you can't do gigs you don't get on TV, and if you don't get on TV you don't get in the papers,' said Matt, slumping back even further in the chair – it was so soft, it was as though it had been upholstered in marshmallows.

'Exactly,' said Mr Pavey. 'And you first hit the headlines with your performance on *The P Factor*—'

'*T Factor*, sir,' corrected Matt.

'It's not important what the show is called, Mills,' snapped Mr Pavey. 'The fact is, when you were famous we were overrun with enquiries from parents interested in their children coming to the school where the young stand-up comic and star of the – what was it? *C Factor*?'

'T, sir,' said Matt. Was it really so difficult to remember one letter?

'Yes. And many of the enquiries were from, how shall I put it . . .' said Mr Pavey, drumming his fingers on his desk, 'a higher calibre of parent than usual. Doctors. Lawyers. Dentists . . . Even, dare I say it, the niece of Norman Jennings, the regional manager of Stonebridge Wells's Rotary Club!'

'I'm not sure what a Rotary Club is, sir,' said Matt, imagining it was something to do with cooking chickens over a fire.

'Well, they do a lot of very important work – I'm a member, albeit at a very junior level, and I'm looking to get a leg up . . . Yes, back when you were a somebody, we were giving St Winifred's a run for their money!'

It started to dawn on Matt what this meeting was really about.

'Have you seen our latest Oftsed report?' barked Mr P, reaching into his desk drawer, retrieving a fat sheaf of papers and slapping it on his desk. He didn't wait for an answer. 'Well, it was not great, not great at all. We're bumping along the bottom of the Kent league tables. That's why we need some other reason for parents to want to send their children here. You were our star attraction, Matt.' Mr Pavey tossed the thick sheaf of papers into the wastepaper basket. 'What's in the pipeline?' he snapped, sitting forward and fixing Matt with a wild-eyed stare.

'Pipeline, sir?' said Matt.

'Yes, pipeline! Any chat shows? TV appearances? What about *Breakfast with Tubbs* – you did very well on that last time, as I remember?'

'No, sir, Mr Tubbs doesn't do that show any more so—'

'Pathetic!' said Mr P, slamming his fist on his desk, and whining as a sharp pain shot up his arm. 'You need to get on the telly,' he bellowed, leaning over the desk, his face bright red in what Matt and Rob called his 'full beetroot mode'.

'I'm keeping an eye on you, Mills. I want to see bookings. TV spots. Mentions in the paper. Or there'll be trouble.'

Matt gulped hard. 'I'll do my best, sir,' he said.

That was all he needed, he thought – as if he wasn't under enough pressure, without being blamed for the school's bad performance in the league tables.

'GO!' barked Mr Pavey. 'And on your way out send the next pupil in.'

Matt made it to the door as quickly as he could without running. He opened the door, and standing there was Kitty Hope.

'Oh, hi, Matt,' said Kitty, a little surprised. 'What kind of mood's he in?'

'Not good,' said Matt. 'Not good at all.'

8

A New Boss for Ian

'Hey, you know that big house you've always had your eye on?' said Ian that evening over dinner.

'Surandon House? The mock-Tudor mansion down the lane by the station?' asked Matt's mum, loading up her fork with mashed potato, suddenly all ears.

'Why is it only Tudor buildings that we mock?' thought Matt, and reached for his little black book – it seemed to him that there might be a gag in that somewhere.

'Yes. Guess who's moved into it?'

'Kim Kardashian?' said Matt dryly. 'I can just see her popping into Martin's the newsagent's for her copy of *OK!*.' As he said this, he started writing in his little black book. He jotted 'Famous people in tiny villages – Elton John in ladies hairdressers, Rita Ora in fish and chip shop, Prince William and Kate in Piece-A-Pizza.'

'It's been bought by my new boss, the owner of Castle Estates – Ted Castle! So whoever says there's no money in estate agency is wrong. He's coming over from South Africa – he's lived there for years.'

'So he's moving into the area then?' said Matt's mum, suddenly distracted from her sausage and mash.

'Apparently,' said Ian. 'Which means he'll be sticking his nose into our branch more often, which can only be bad news for yours truly.'

'Not necessarily – why don't you invite him round, get him onside? You never know, you might get a promotion – we could certainly do with the money,' she said.

'Invite him round here?' scoffed Ian. 'I don't think so. But he's got a son your age, Matt. He's starting at Anglebrook School after the Easter break. And Ted's keen for the pair of you to meet up beforehand so we've all been invited round to the big house this weekend. He said for you to bring some friends too – you know, give the boy a head start, so when he starts school he will at least know a few faces. What do think?'

'Bit lame,' said Matt. 'Maybe I'll arrange for you to meet up with some strangers on your day off.'

'Now, Matt, that's not very nice!' said his mum crossly. 'Put yourself in this boy's position. No, you tell Rob and Ahmed that the three of you will be going.'

'Don't fancy that much,' said Rob when Matt told him Ian's plan.

'Yeah, count me out,' said Ahmed. 'I ain't interested. I don't have any vacancies for friends at the moment. All positions are filled – unless you're a girl and your name's Ayeesha, that is.'

'That's what I thought you'd say,' moaned Matt.

Saturday morning came round quickly. Matt was dragging his feet getting ready for the barbecue at

Ted Castle's mock-Tudor manor house when the doorbell rang.

'Answer that, Matt, would you?' called Ian from upstairs.

Matt opened the door and standing there were Rob and Ahmed.

'What are you doing here?' said Matt. 'I'm off out to that dopey barbecue.'

'We know,' said Rob.

'We're coming with you to meet the kid in the big house,' said Ahmed with a pained look on his face.

'But I thought—' said Matt.

'I took the liberty of having a word with Deborah and Mona,' said Matt's mum, appearing behind him in the doorway. 'Glad you could make it, boys! Come in. We won't be a minute, Ian's doing his hair!'

'Ha!' laughed Matt, closing the door behind them as they stepped into the front room. 'So your mums leaned on you too?'

'Yeah,' said Rob. 'It was either this or being grounded for the weekend.'

'It won't be that bad, lads,' said Ian, breezing through the door dressed in a rather garish Hawaiian shirt and khaki shorts. 'Apparently they've got a heated swimming pool, a jacuzzi and a home cinema with a four-metre wide screen – so it could be worse. How do I look?' He turned to face the boys, who immediately let out a cackle.

'Wot?' said Ian, affronted.

'Ha! What have you done to your hair?' said Matt. 'It looks like you didn't brush it, you polished it instead!'

Ian rolled his eyes. 'I put some gel on it to try to get it to lie flat. You know the trouble I have with my hair, it's got a life of its own. At school they used to call me The Frizz!'

'Oh dear,' said Matt's mum, joining them from the kitchen. 'What's happened here?' she said, poking his hair gingerly with a finger and getting a globule of gel on it. 'Yuk! What have you got on your hair?'

'Oh, not you as well,' opined Ian, putting his hands on his hips.

'It looks like you've just finished a shift at the fish and chip shop,' she continued. 'You'd better go and rinse it off, quick.'

'There isn't time,' said Ian, looking at his watch. 'We're already fifteen minutes late.'

'Well, you'd better put a hat on then,' she trilled, rummaging around in the hall and returning with a straw trilby. 'Pop that on, and whatever you do, don't take it off!'

9

Barbecue Beef

'It's down here somewhere,' said Ian ten minutes later, manoeuvring the Astra along a narrow tree-lined lane.

'Blimey, their drive is longer than our road!' said Rob from his position on the back seat, wedged in between Matt and Ahmed. The road surface became gravelly as they turned a corner, and suddenly there it was – a huge house, the white walls cut into squares, rectangles and triangles by dark wooden beams, with green wisteria growing above the front door.

As the car pulled up outside, the front door opened

and two huge Great Danes bounded out to meet them. They jumped up – one sprawled its giant frame across the bonnet, the other appeared to be trying to climb on to the roof.

'It's like we're on safari in a pet shop!' said Matt, reaching for his little black book again.

'Don't worry, they're perfectly harmless,' came a voice with a thick South African accent from the doorway. Matt peered through the car window, through the giant legs of the Great Dane, to see a tall man in his late thirties with dark hair. He had a light tan, very white teeth and where Ian had a slight pot belly, this man looked extremely toned.

'Tanned and toned!' thought Matt. That pretty much summed this man up.

'Hi, Ted,' said Ian, winding down the window. Both dogs had their paws up against the roof of the Astra and were rocking it back and forth. 'Can you call 'em off? I'm worried about my paintwork!'

Ted Castle chuckled, put his fingers up to his mouth and let out a loud whistle. The dogs dropped from the car, raced over to join him and sat obediently at his feet.

'You must excuse Nelson and Winnie,' he said, walking across to the new arrivals. 'They're just very friendly.' He leaned down and opened the passenger door. 'Mrs Mills, welcome to Surandon House! Ian's told me all about you. Did you bring the dachshunds?' he said, graciously helping Matt's mum out of the car.

'I thought it best to leave them,' said Matt's mum, blushing slightly. 'Given the size difference!'

Mr Castle laughed again and then opened the door to the back seat of the car. 'I'm Ted,' he said and shook each of the boys' hands as they got out. 'Now, which one of you is Matt? No, don't tell me,' he said surveying them.

'I'll give you a clue,' said Ahmed dryly. 'It's not me.' Ted smiled.

'I'm Matt,' said Matt.

'Hi, Matt,' said Ted, then looked over at Ian as if comparing them. 'He doesn't look much like you, Ian!'

'Hmm, there's a reason for that,' muttered Ian.

'Ian's had extensive plastic surgery on his face, Mr James. Yes, he doesn't like to talk about it but he's in a witness protection scheme and was given a whole new identity – oops, I wasn't supposed to tell you that!' laughed Matt.

'You're definitely Matt then. I heard you were a bit of a joker,' chuckled Ted.

'A bit of a joker?' exclaimed Rob, digging Matt in the ribs. 'This is Matt Millz, the youngest stand-up comedian in the world!'

'Ahem,' said Ian. 'I brought you a bottle of wine, Ted,' he said, trying to move the conversation on.

'It's only screw-top but it said in the paper it tastes of orange and pecans, so . . . Oh, and a bunch of flowers for Mrs C.'

'Did I hear someone mention my name?' said a pretty blonde woman walking across the gravel drive to join them. 'Hello, boys,' she said. 'I hope you brought your swimming things? Why don't you go and join James – he's by the pool.'

The boys looked at each other awkwardly.

'Go ahead,' said Mr Castle. 'Through the front door and out the back. You can't miss it – it's big and blue and very wet!'

'Wow! Look at this place!' said Ahmed, gazing around in wonder as they walked through the house towards the French doors that opened on to the back garden. 'They must be minted!'

'Yeah,' said Rob. 'Change of career – if anyone asks, from now on I want to be an estate agent!'

They were right. If the exterior of the house harked back to the time of Henry the Eighth, the inside was bang up to date. It had low white-leather sofas and on the walls there were paintings and prints that Matt felt sure he'd seen in books and magazines. Through the French windows to the right of the pool was a wooden bar area with high stools around it.

'It's like a five-star hotel!' marvelled Matt.

As they stepped on to the patio, a boy's face peered round one of the sun loungers.

'Hi,' said the boy, getting up. 'I'm James, but most people call me Jamie.' His accent wasn't quite as marked as his dad's but there was a bit of a South African twang. He was roughly the same height as Matt although a little fuller in the shoulders, the physique of someone who swam regularly. He had thick short black hair cut in a rather old-fashioned short back and sides, and dark eyebrows over blue eyes. His face was tanned and a few freckles speckled his cheeks. He was wearing a white towelling robe with 'Jamie' embroidered on it in gold lettering and all three of the boys – without exception – took an instant dislike to him.

'So, Jamie, let's cut to the chase. Your dad must be worth a bomb to be able to afford a place like this!' said Ahmed.

Jamie laughed. 'Yeah, embarrassing, isn't it? He even makes me wear this dumb robe with my name on it!' he said. Suddenly the atmosphere changed and the boys relaxed. The fact that he was able to take the mickey out of himself was a very good sign.

'Hi, Jamie,' said Matt, stepping forward to shake the boy's hand. 'I'm Matt.'

'Yes, I know. I saw you on *The T Factor*. I thought you were brilliant,' said Jamie.

'Oh dear!' said Rob, slapping his forehead in mock exasperation. 'He's a Matt Millz fan! Security!'

Jamie looked at the floor awkwardly, not knowing quite how to react.

'Thanks, Jamie,' said Matt, extremely pleased that someone at least

remembered his finest hour. 'Nice to meet someone with such great taste in comedy,' he said giving Rob a playful shove. 'Seems like a long time ago!'

'Are you doing any more gigs . . . ? I'd like to come along if you are,' continued Jamie.

'Bit of a sore point,' said Ahmed, shaking his head dramatically.

Matt shoved his hands deep into his pockets and shrugged disconsolately. 'Nothing on the horizon, I'm afraid. That whole time seems to be a bit of a dream to me now . . .'

'Boo-hoo-hoo!' cried Rob, pulling out a hanky and mopping his eyes in mock sorrow. 'My career's over and I'm only twelve!'

'Thirteen actually,' said Matt chuckling, seeing the funny side. 'See what I have to put up with, Jamie? And he's supposed to be my friend!'

'You haven't told me your names,' said Jamie.

'Sorry, I'm Rob,' said Rob, shaking Jamie's hand.

'And I'm Ahmed,' said Ahmed.

'Do you want some crisps?' Jamie asked, gesturing

to a long table under an awning that was laden with bowls of salad and bread and cold meats and crisps. 'Yeah, Mum went a bit over the top. I think she was expecting the whole class!'

The boys grabbed a handful of crisps while Jamie fetched them some drinks – tiny cans of their favourite fizzy drink.

They had a splash around in the pool for a while, then Matt found himself with Jamie alone. 'What other comics do you like then, Jamie?' said Matt.

'It's a pretty long list,' said Jamie. 'Michael McIntyre?'

Matt nodded.

'John Bishop, Jason Manford, Lee Mack . . .'

'Oh, so more the observational types?'

'Huh?' said Jamie.

'Oh, you know, observational comedians. They tend to pick up on stuff that we've all seen but never really noticed, you know – like Michael McIntyre's routine about revolving doors. We've all seen that, all experienced it, but it's only when he points it out we kind of realise how dumb it is, and mainly if something's dumb it's funny.'

'Especially the way he does it,' said Jamie.

'Yeah, I guess. I prefer the crazier ones. The silly stuff.'

'Yeah? Who's in your top three?'

'Well, number one is easy – Eddie Odillo,' said Matt.

'Yeah? He's good. I'm not sure I get all of it though . . .' said Jamie.

'Oh, he's the man as far as I'm concerned. Ever seen him live?'

Jamie shook his head.

'Ah, well, live he's something else. I mean, he's funny on TV, but live . . . Ever tried it?' said Matt.

'What?' said Jamie.

'Stand-up. Ever had a go?'

'Oh no,' said Jamie with a laugh in his voice. 'Don't get me wrong, I love performing, you know, acting – I did a lot of school plays at my last school, but stand-up? I'm happy to do someone else's lines but the idea of making up the whole thing? Nah, not for me.'

'You should try it,' said Matt. 'It's not so different to acting you know.'

'It was nice, but it wasn't like a home, was it?' said Ian as they made their way back up the drive to join the road.

'No, it was better!' said Matt.

'It wasn't like my home, that's for sure,' said Ahmed, and they all laughed.

'A house like that would be a devil of a job to keep clean,' said Matt's mum.

'Yes,' laughed Ian. 'Particularly if you never bother to clean it!'

Matt's mum laughed along through gritted teeth. 'I think they have help,' she said.

'How was Jamie?' said Ian. 'Think he'll fit in OK at Anglebrook?'

'You know, I wasn't sure about him at first,' said Matt, 'but actually, he's OK. Yeah, I think he's gonna fit in just fine.'

And Ahmed and Rob agreed.

Jamie did fit in very well. Most breaks he'd meet up with Rob, Matt and Ahmed and help them chew the fat on the steps outside the science block, and more often than not he'd accompany them to Greggs in the lunch break or after school.

He didn't quite have the same sense of humour as them – he wasn't as quick off the mark when it came to a gag – but Matt liked him and he always had plenty of spare change in his pocket when it came to buying jumbo sausage rolls, which helped.

10

Better Late Than Never

'A little present for you!' said Matt's mum, exchanging a smile and a wink with Ian and handing him an envelope.

'What's this? My birthday was months ago!' said Matt, tearing it open. Inside were five theatre tickets. 'Tickets?' he said.

'Well, have a look at them then,' said Ian giving him a nudge.

Matt flipped them over. *Eddie Odillo Live at the London Palladium* they screamed. 'Wow!' he exclaimed.

'Think of it as a late birthday present,' said his mum.

'Or an early Christmas present!' said Ian.

'It was Ian's idea – he thought you needed cheering up.'

Ian nodded. 'Well, I know the whole comedy thing has hit the buffers a bit . . .'

Matt winced at Ian's rather blunt assessment but he had to agree. 'Hit the buffers? Derailed and hit a brick wall more like,' said Matt, rolling his eyes.

'So Ian thought you might like to see a real expert at work,' said Matt's mum brightly.

'No, Jenny, that's not what I said,' said Ian, giving his wife a sharp dig in the ribs. 'What I said was, Matt loves his comedy and you know, it might inspire him to . . .' He tailed off.

'Great!' said Matt. 'I've only ever seen Eddie Odillo do twenty-minute slots in clubs – I've never seen his full show. *Five* tickets though?'

'Yes, well, Ian will take you – it's not really my sort of thing – so you can take three friends.'

'Decent!' said Matt, nodding his head and tucking the tickets back into the envelope. If he couldn't be up on that stage he might as well watch a master at work.

11

Masterclass

It was just a short walk from Oxford Circus tube down Argyll Street to possibly the most famous theatre in the western world – the London Palladium, the high church of light entertainment.

Matt looked up at the grand white-stone portico above the entrance. Guarding the gold doors were two men in red tailcoats and top hats.

'Looks like a palace,' he muttered under his breath.

'In some ways it is,' said Kitty, equally in awe.

The ushers inspected their tickets and they walked up the red-carpeted stairs, through the gold and glass doors and into the equally glittering foyer.

It was packed with people of all shapes and sizes, from young teens like Matt and his friends to whole families and even a few elderly couples.

'The fact that Eddie's doing his own thing and appealing to such a broad audience is so cool,' said Kitty, taking in the crowd.

As they followed the signs for the dress circle up a marble staircase, she grabbed Matt's hand and turned to Ian. 'Excuse me, Mr Woodwood, is it OK if I take Matt off for a couple of seconds? I just want to show him something. You know my grandad used to run this place.'

'Here we go again,' joked Rob, with a sideways smirk at Ahmed. Then he mimicked her voice: *'Did you know my grandad was Bernie Hopestein who was the most successful man in showbiz who ever lived!'*

Matt gave him a shove.

'Er, I think you have mentioned that before, Kitty . . .' said Ian patiently, looking around for their row of seats. 'That's fine, as long as the pair of you are back in ten minutes for the start of the show.' He tapped his watch.

'Of course,' she said brightly, leading Matt towards a red velvet curtain to the side of the dress circle.

'Where are you taking me?' said a rather confused Matt, dragging his feet, looking back over his shoulder at the audience taking their seats. 'We don't want to miss any of it!'

'My grandad showed me this route; hopefully it still works . . .' she said, pushing the curtain aside to reveal a door with a series of buttons below the handle, a combination lock of some sort.

'Ah, that's floored your little plan,' said Matt. 'Let's get back.'

'You're right . . .' said Kitty, scratching her chin. 'Unless they haven't changed the code since I was last here . . .' With that she punched at four or five of the buttons with her index finger and tugged at the handle. To the amazement of them both, the door swung open. Kitty turned to Matt triumphantly and the pair of them pushed on through the door, closing it behind them.

The bright gold and red of the auditorium gave way to a more utilitarian decor – flat white walls and lino floor, with fluorescent strip lighting above them leading off down a corridor towards another door. 'Come on,' said Kitty, scuttling down the corridor. 'We haven't got long!'

Matt ran after her, intrigued.

They went through the next door and were confronted by a set of steep steps. At the top was another, much heavier metal door, it looked like some sort of emergency exit with patches of rust at the edges where it met the door frame. There was a large but faded sign on it: THEATRE PERSONNEL ONLY.

'Ah,' said Matt. 'It says theatre personnel only, so that's us out then . . .'

'Oh, come on,' said Kitty. 'We've got this far!' She grabbed the bar across the door that served as its handle and pushed at it with her full weight, but it didn't budge. She tried again – still nothing. 'Well, don't just stand there, give me a hand,' she said.

'I really do think we should be getting back …' said Matt, then he took a step back and lurched forwards, putting his shoulder to the door. There was a grinding sound, then a clunk and a loud creak as the door swung open, pitching the pair forward. They both fell, front first, on to the cold damp floor. Was it a floor? It felt sort of gritty and smelled strongly of tar.

'Where are we?' said Matt, staggering to his feet and trying to get his bearings. He looked up and was surprised to see the night sky. Ahead of him was a low wall that continued all around them – and above that the whole of London was laid out in front of them. They were on the roof!

'Pretty cool, eh?' said Kitty, exceptionally pleased with herself. 'Look over there – you can just see the top of Buckingham Palace, and behind you, that's the BT tower and beyond that the Gherkin!'

'Wow!' said Matt, spinning round, taking it all

in – the lights, the higgledy-piggledy silhouettes of buildings, the domes of churches and palaces, the square blocks of skyscrapers. Beyond them, set in the dark navy sky above the smog, only the brightest of the night's stars shone through. It never really gets dark in London – there's always the hazy orange tint of street lamps and car headlights diffusing up from below.

In front of them there was the silhouette of a huge triangle that Matt realised instantly was the very

portico he'd walked under just moments ago on their way in.

They ran to it and peered over. There directly below them was London's West End. 'It's literally glittering!' he exclaimed.

'What's that?' said Kitty, her face lit up from below.

'They always describe the West End as "London's glittering West End" – well, tonight I can see why!'

Kitty nodded then suddenly turned serious. 'Listen, Matt,' she said, 'I know things haven't turned out quite the way we'd hoped . . .'

'It's a tough business, I understand that,' he replied, looking out over Oxford Street towards Hyde Park. 'I mean, it's not your fault. I am only thirteen . . . so . . .'

'Well, I just wanted you to know that I still believe in you, that I haven't given up and that I'm still trying for you.' Kitty turned to face him. Matt looked at her, then stepped forward and gave her a hug.

There was a low rumble that rose up through the roof and through their feet.

'What on earth's that?' said Matt.

'That's applause!' exclaimed Kitty. 'The show must have started! We'd better get back!'

In their excitement they'd almost forgotten what they were doing at the Palladium in the first place!

They looked at each other, laughed and dashed towards the metal door.

'Where have you been?' hissed Ian, tapping his watch as Matt and Kitty made their away along the row to their seats. The other audience members groaned as they stood up to let them pass. 'Ow!' yelped a big burly man as Matt accidentally trod on his foot.

'Sorry,' said Matt

'You've missed the first five minutes,' said Ian.

'It's only the support act,' chipped in Ahmed. 'And he's pretty lame.'

'Give him a chance,' hissed Rob as the person in the row in front turned to shush them.

'Sorry, Ian. Kitty took me up on the roof,' said Matt.

'Will I ever get a straight answer out of you?'

said Ian, rolling his eyes. 'Anyway, you're here now – fancy a Malteser?' he asked, poking a red box under his nose. Matt took a couple and settled back to enjoy the show.

Sadly, Ahmed was right about the support act – it was fairly run-of-the-mill observational stuff.

'Hey! Have you noticed the difference between cats and dogs?' said the tubby comic.

Matt looked at Rob and they both rolled their eyes.

There were a few pools of laughter and a respectable smattering of applause as he announced the interval and left the stage after about forty minutes.

'Who wants an ice cream?' said Ian, getting up to stretch his legs. As he reached into his pocket for some money, Rob jumped to his feet.

'I'll get them,' he said, waving a twenty-pound note. 'My mum gave me some money and told me to get the snacks. Who wants what?'

They gave Rob their orders and he and Ahmed went off to join the queue for ice cream.

'Why would Eddie book such a ropey support act?' said Matt, turning to Kitty.

'Ah, well, booking a support act is a tricky thing,' she said sagely. 'I mean, you don't want someone who's too funny ...'

'Too funny?'

'Yes, the last thing you want is the audience liking them more than you, the main act!'

Matt smiled and nodded; he could see the sense in that.

'You want a comic who makes the main act look even better than they actually are, but not someone who's so bad they wind up the crowd and make them feel like they've been cheated. I'd say our friend there pretty much fitted the bill – and don't forget it's a pretty thankless task. No one's come to see him – everyone was just biding their time until Eddie comes on.'

'I'd never thought of it like that,' said Matt. Once again Kitty was bang on the money.

Ahmed appeared looking a little flustered.

'Er, Mr ... er ... I mean, Ian, have you got a spare couple of quid – it's just that the ice creams were more than Rob's mum thought,' he said.

Ian smiled and handed him a ten-pound note. 'It's daylight robbery,' he muttered.

'It's not actually,' chirped up Matt with a smirk. 'It's dark outside, it's night-time robbery!'

Pretty soon Ahmed and Rob returned.

'Honestly,' said Ian, inspecting his change. 'Five pounds for a tiny tub of ice cream? Someone's making a lot of money tonight ...'

Just then the music started to get louder and as the lights dimmed the audience sat forward in their seats expectantly. There was an almost palpable feeling of excitement in the room as they all waited to see their hero.

'What an atmosphere,' whispered Kitty. Matt nodded.

'Ladies and gentlemen,' came a deep voice with a silly fake American accent that Matt was pretty sure he recognised. 'One or two announcements before we begin. During the parrot display we do ask you not to approach the birds as they are extremely nervous and may forget their words!'

The audience laughed.

Matt and Rob looked at each other. 'Parrot display?' they said simultaneously.

'And in the event of a fire ... well, we've had it basically!' said the voice, the accent slipping slightly, to another laugh even bigger than the one before. 'We are toast! Look at this place, it's made from wood and fabric. It's an accident waiting to happen!'

Then it dawned on Matt. 'It's him,' he whispered to Kitty. 'It's Eddie!'

'Yes,' she said. 'Amazing! He's getting laughs before he's even come on!'

Then the comedian dropped the accent completely. 'Nah! Only kidding! It's me!' There was a ripple of applause. 'But I'm scared,' he said with a mock whimper. 'I'm too scared to come on!'

'Ah!' went the crowd, playing along with the gag.

'Is it OK if I do the act from behind the curtain

tonight? It's just that I've got a big zit on top of my head and I'm afraid it's going to burst!' Another big laugh.

'Come on out, Eddie! We want to see you!' shrieked a woman down the front of the stalls.

'Mum?' said Eddie. 'I thought I told you to wait in the car!'

A huge laugh – made even funnier by the shrieking of the woman in the front row.

'Listen. OK, I'll come out but only if you promise not to laugh.'

'That's a brilliant line,' thought Matt. Here was a comedian telling the audience not to do the very thing they'd all turned up to do. Priceless!

'Do you promise not to laugh?'

'We promise, Eddie!' shrieked the woman down the front, only this time she was joined by half the audience.

'OK, if you promise, here I come!'

With that the curtains opened and out walked Eddie, to a huge round of applause and cheering.

On top of his head he had what looked like a fifty-centimetre giant zit!

'Hey,' said Eddie, acting all hurt. 'You promised you wouldn't laugh!' This made the audience laugh even harder. 'You promised,' protested Eddie, barely able to suppress a huge smile.

'Oh dear, I guess I'll just have to give it a squeeze!' With that he placed both hands up around the 'spot' and squeezed it. A huge jet of white foam shot out of the top and hit the front two rows.

'Yup, that seems to have got it,' he said.

There was a huge round of applause and a cheer and the comedian whipped the fake zit off the top of his head.

'Hey!' He pulled his trademark face. 'How's everyone doing?' There was another big cheer. 'Check

me out at the Palladium,' he said, affecting a cocky attitude, strolling up and down the stage with a swagger like he owned the place. Then he promptly fell off the front of the stage into the orchestra pit! A split second later he bounced back up, off a hidden trampoline.

By now the audience were in hysterics. Matt looked around at their faces – flushed red, eyes bulging, some gasping for air. 'How on earth can he keep this going for ninety minutes?' he wondered.

But Eddie did. There were runs of short gags creating huge bursts of laughter, like at the top of the show. Then these would be followed by longer bits, which would draw the crowd in, a shaggy-dog story perhaps, Eddie pretending that he was confiding in them. They'd be thinking he was telling them a true story, something candid about himself and then – KAPOW! – he'd turn the story on its head, pull the rug from under them and they'd be rolling about in fits of laughter again.

He seemed to know exactly what to do, where

to stand, what face to pull, when to hold back and when to press on with the laughs until the audience were rendered helpless. In short, he was an expert. By the time he'd finished his set and left the stage, the audience were on their feet and begging for more. He walked back on briefly, thanked them for coming, waved and was off again.

'No encore?' said Rob.

'Always leave 'em wanting more, Rob,' said Kitty.

Matt nodded. 'That was brilliant, thanks, Ian,' he said, standing and putting his coat on.

'Yes, thanks, Ian,' said the others.

'It's not over yet, Matt,' said Ian with a broad grin.

'Not over?' quizzed Matt. 'What do you mean?'

'You'll find out if you follow me,' said Ian, heading off towards the exit. For some reason he looked incredibly pleased with himself.

Matt and his friends shrugged and fell in line behind him. As they got to the next level down, one of the Palladium ushers came to meet them. Ian leaned in and whispered something in the usher's ear, the man nodded and led them through another door with a combination lock on it, like the one Kitty had cracked, and suddenly they were backstage.

'What's going on?' said Matt.

'Just shut up and follow me,' grinned Ian as they were led off the stage, through some old double doors, along a shiny painted brickwork corridor towards . . . could it be? Yes! It was a room with a gold star on it, so it had to be a dressing room. Finally it dawned on Matt. They were going to meet the star of the show. They were going to meet Eddie Odillo!

'OMG!' said Rob.

The usher knocked on the door, twisted the handle and they entered. And there he was! Eddie was sitting at the dressing-room table, scanning through his set list, a towel round his shoulders, his stage shirt soaked in sweat. When he saw Matt, his face broke into a big smile and he jumped up to shake his hand.

'Matt Millz!' he cried, greeting the boy like an old friend.

'That was ... I mean that was ...' Matt was lost for words – so Ahmed stepped in to help him out.

'Awesome!' said Ahmed.

'Brilliant!' said Rob

'Knockout!' said Ian

'Hey! There's no words left for me,' said Matt. 'But truly, that was the best I've ever seen you, Eddie!'

'He's right,' said Kitty, stepping forward. 'You get better and better with every tour!'

'Kitty, right?' said Eddie, stooping to shake her hand. 'Well, you know I prefer to do my own thing rather than be on the bill with a load of other comics,' he said, dragging the towel across his forehead.

'Yeah?' said Matt, eager to pick up any insights into a successful career in comedy.

'Don't tell the producers of *Stand-up at the Apollo* that,' smirked Ian.

But Eddie brushed off the comment with a shrug. Matt could see that behind the jokey facade he was deadly serious about his craft. 'Yes, with my own show I can set the tone from the beginning – I don't have to follow some guy who bombs or is too funny.'

'No danger of that, Eddie. Really it was just great, and thanks for letting us come backstage,' said Ian. He turned to Matt and his friends. 'Now we'd better leave this gentleman to his family.'

'Matt'll catch you up,' said Eddie putting his arm on Matt's shoulder and taking him to one corner of the dressing room. Ian nodded and herded the others out through the door.

'So, how's it going?' said the older comic. 'I haven't heard much about you for a while.'

'That's just it – it's not going anywhere,' said Matt dolefully.

'No? Trouble getting gigs, huh?' said Eddie.

'You bet. I can't get arrested. There's no gigs round where I live ...'

'Where's that, remind me?'

'Kent – out in the country.'

'Ah.'

'I did the five-minute open spot at the Comedy Store and Mr Wardle told me to come back in six months for another one. Six months!'

'Listen, there are no short cuts. It takes what it takes – you're so young, Matt,' said Eddie gently.

'So everyone keeps telling me,' moaned Matt.

'You've just got to keep at it.'

'At what, though? There is no "it", I'm dead in the water.'

'Writing, thinking up bits, knocking on doors. You think I just walked into dressing-room number one at the London Palladium?'

'No, but . . .'

'No. Believe me, it took ten years to get here, and you know how many gigs I did in my first year as a stand-up?'

Matt shrugged – he had no idea. 'Forty? Fifty?'

'Three. Three gigs – I died twice, but the third one got me a booking, and that's how it works. The next year I did twenty gigs, the third year I was working virtually every night. It just takes time. These days it's even harder – every Tom, Dick and Harry wants to be a comedian.'

'Don't you mean Harriet?' said Matt.

'Huh?' said Eddie

'There's loads of girls going into comedy now too.'

'You're right – it's harder than it ever was, so you've just got to be patient.' Eddie put a hand on each of Matt's shoulders and looked Matt squarely in the eyes. 'I wouldn't say this to just anyone, but I know you've got talent. If you want it badly enough, it's yours. Promise me you won't give up.'

Matt looked away, slightly embarrassed. 'Yeah, OK,' he mumbled.

'Sorry, didn't hear that?' said Eddie, looking a little cross.

'I promise I won't give up,' Matt repeated.

'That's better, now you'd better go and catch up with your dad,' he said, letting Matt go.

'Thanks, Eddie, I really appreciate it,' said Matt.

As Matt made his way back towards the front of the Palladium he recognised the corridor that he and Kitty had gone down earlier, the one that led to the roof. He looked around for a split second, then ran down it, through the door, then bounded up the stairs, flung open the big rusty iron door and burst out on to the roof of the Palladium once again. He stood at the apex above the grand entrance and looked out over London as it twinkled below him, as theatres emptied and groups of people went in search of fun, and at the top of his voice he shouted his new mantra.

'I'M A COMEDIAN AND I WILL NEVER GIVE UP!'

12

Fringe Benefits

The next morning Matt woke up with a renewed sense of purpose. He was buzzing almost as much as if it had been him on stage the night before. He was brimming with ideas for gags and routines. The only thing he didn't have any idea about was how to get himself some stage time.

'Help me, Kit! Any chance we can have a chat about my future?' he said in a text to Kitty at first break.

'I've had an idea,' she texted back. 'See you in the DMC after school.'

As Matt made his way there later, he saw something

that surprised him. Mr Gillingham's battered old Volkswagen Beetle was pulled up outside the school and Miss Jolly – the new drama teacher – got out, walked round to the driver's side to where Mr Gillingham was sitting, leaned into the window and gave him a big kiss ... on the lips!

'Wow!' muttered Matt with a grin, ducking behind a brick wall. 'Mr G's got himself a girlfriend!'

'You'll never guess what I've just seen,' he said as he walked into the DMC to see Kitty.

'Can it wait, Matt? I really need to tell you my idea,' she said. She looked really pleased with herself and immediately had Matt's attention. 'I got it last night reading Eddie's biog in this,' she said, waving the Eddie Odillo souvenir tour programme at him. Matt took it and flicked through it – not for the first time. He'd read it from cover to cover twice after he'd got home from the gig.

'What about his biog?' said Matt, scanning it once again for any clues.

EDDIE ODILLO

Born 1985 in Lagos, Nigeria. Moved to London when he was five. Parents both teachers. One brother.

Early years – quickly made a name for himself on the London comedy circuit.

Won the Wetfizz Best Newcomer Award at the Edinburgh Fringe Festival 2013, First National Tour 2014 'Nutz!'.

Eddie has made regular appearances on *Scoff at the Week* (BBC2), *Eight Out of Ten Comics* (C4) and *Stand-up at the Apollo* – started hosting in 2017. *Eddie Odillo Stand-up* 2018 (Netflix), *Eddie's Road Trip to Africa* (ITV) 2019.

'I don't know what you're getting at,' said Matt, perplexed.

Kitty snatched it back and started reading it out to him: '"Won the Wetfizz Best Newcomer Award at the Edinburgh Fringe Festival"...' She stopped reading and looked at Matt expectantly.

'The Edinburgh ...?'

'The Edinburgh Fringe Festival! Don't you see?'

'Edinburgh Festival ... That's Scotland, isn't it? I remember Mr G mentioned something about it, which reminds me I saw him and—'

'It's a whole month of shows.'

'What is?'

'The Edinburgh Fringe,' she said, snatching the programme back from him.

'Yeah, great, but there's no way they'd book me,' said Matt, shaking his head, a frown knotting his forehead.

'But that's just it,' Kitty exclaimed. 'You don't have to get booked. Anyone can do it!'

'What do you mean, anyone can do it? Someone

must be in charge. There must be some quality control, surely?' said Matt.

'No, literally anyone can do it provided they've got the money.'

'Wait a minute – you're telling me I could do a gig every night for four weeks?'

'Yes,' she said excitedly. 'Although that would cost a fortune, so I'm thinking two weeks.'

'Two weeks of gigs,' repeated Matt. 'Well, how do we sign up? What do we have to do to be a part of this Edinburgh Festival?'

'All we need to do is get a venue and pay our registration fee with the Fringe Office!' she said with a broad grin.

'Well, what are waiting for? How much does it come to? What's it gonna cost?' said Matt.

'Well, I've done a bit of research and a few sums,' said Kitty, spreading out some printed A4 sheets on the top of the desk. 'Now, assuming we can get some others to come too – Neil, maybe Alex or someone else – you know, put on a show of three acts with maybe a compere, we can spread the costs – I'll pay a share too obviously . . .'

'How much?' said Matt.

'According to my calculations – if we don't go for the most central venue and limit the amount of publicity we do . . . Plus we'd need somewhere to stay . . .'

'How much?' said Matt, detecting a potential problem.

'And obviously any cost is offset by ticket sales . . . Plus, you never know, we could look at getting sponsorship . . .' said Kitty sheepishly.

'How much?' repeated Matt a little more firmly.

'Somewhere in the region of . . . twelve hundred pounds,' she said.

Matt took a moment to think about it. 'Well . . . OK, I suppose twelve hundred pounds between five of us isn't too bad. I've got about sixty quid left over from my birthday money and—'

'Each,' said Kitty sheepishly. 'That's twelve hundred pounds each. And that's not including the cost of food . . .'

'Twelve hundred pounds each?' Matt exclaimed. 'And that's if we don't eat anything! Where am I going to get that sort of money? Where are any of us going to get that sort of money? I mean we don't all live in big houses like Jamie, Kit!'

'I know, I know,' she said, trying to calm him down. 'But like I say, if we sell out, we'd make money, only a small amount, but compared to the value of the experience and the stage time, you've got to see it as an investment in your future.'

Matt let out a huge sigh and ran his hand through his quiff. 'I get all that,' he groaned. 'You don't have to sell that bit to me. Believe me, I'd sell my right arm to get two weeks of gigs – I mean, the only problem then would be I'd have to hold the mic in my left hand but … twelve hundred pounds? It's a fortune!'

Matt turned away from her and stood staring out of the classroom window. If he could get a few odd jobs, and if he had enough time, surely it might be possible … ?

'When's the deadline?' he said, looking back at her.

'Soon,' she said.

'How soon?'

'Two months.'

'Oh, for the love of fudge,' he said, throwing his arms in the air, exasperated. This was maddening. 'Every time I think it might be possible you move the goalposts!' he cried.

Matt looked out of the window, across the playing field at the empty playground.

'Right, well I'd better work out how I'm going to raise that money,' he said, turning and fixing Kitty with a determined look. 'Because one thing's for sure, I'm going to this year's Edinburgh Festival if it kills me!'

13

Funds Not Fun

How do you get your hands on twelve hundred pounds if you're only thirteen years old? Well, Matt calculated that after he'd subtracted his savings and if he didn't spend any of his pocket money from that point on, what he actually needed was nine hundred and thirty-nine pounds and eighty-nine pence.

'Ian? Got any jobs you need doing?' said Matt that evening, as his stepfather arrived home from work.

'Give us a chance to get in, Matt,' he said wearily, plonking his briefcase on the kitchen table, taking off his raincoat and slinging it on the back of a chair. 'What a day. That new boss, Ted Castle – he's a right pain in the—'

'Hello, darling,' squawked Matt's mum, walking into the kitchen and giving Ian a big hug. 'Sit yourself down and I'll put the kettle on. It's your favourite tonight – sausage surprise!'

SAUSAGE SURPRISE!

Ian looked at Matt and pulled a face. They both knew that his mum's cooking was never going to win any prizes but when she came up with her own recipes – as in the case of her so-called sausage surprise – the results were pretty dire. Matt had joked to Ian on a previous occasion that the big surprise about his mum's sausage surprise was that she'd managed to render one of his favourite foods – sausages – into something that was virtually inedible. Even the dogs had refused to eat the copious leftovers from her last attempt.

'Have either of you got any jobs I can do for a little extra pocket money?' said Matt, cutting to the chase.

'Well, you can wash the Astra,' said Ian.

'Good, yes, I can do that. What are you paying?'

'I dunno, three quid?'

'Three quid!?' spluttered Matt. 'Is that all?'

'Well, I can get it done professionally for ten by those Polish blokes next to the office.'

'Ah, but I'll do inside and out,' said Matt.

'That *is* for inside and out – they do a great job and spray that stuff around that's supposed to make it smell like a new car. New Car Spray it's called. Although to be honest what I really need is a spray that makes my job smell like a new one – Mr Castle has introduced all kinds of new quotas and paperwork.'

'Isn't that a bit misleading for a blind person?' said Matt.

'Eh?' said Ian, a confused look on his face.

'Well, I mean, if you were selling the Astra, all you'd need to do is spray it with this new car smell stuff and a blind bloke would take one sniff, think it was new and reckon he'd found a bargain,' said Matt, reaching for his little black book.

'What would a blind person be doing buying a car?' said his mum, who was now busy chopping up some onions.

'Might be a gift, I suppose . . .' said Ian, looking even more confused.

Matt opened his little black book and jotted down 'Sprays that make things smell new' – he'd come back to that later.

'Anyway, how about five quid, in and out, and although I won't be able to make it smell new, I will be able to make it smell . . . er . . . different.'

'Yeah OK, whatever, I like different. Five pounds it is.'

'Great,' said Matt. 'Any other jobs? Mum? Got any jobs I can do for money?'

'Well, jobs is the word – I'll pay you to pick up the dogs' mess in the back garden.'

'Ha ha! I hate that job!' chuckled Ian, cracking open a can of lager and taking a big glug. 'Phew,' he said. 'I needed that.'

Matt hesitated – had it really come to this? Picking up dogs' mess in order to further his comedy career? 'How much?' he said reluctantly.

'You wouldn't get me doing that for all the tea in China. Not after the day I've had,' moaned Ian, shaking his head and taking another slurp of beer. 'Why are some people so obsessed with performance targets?'

'I tell you what, I'll make it performance-related,' said Matt's mum with a giggle. 'I'll give you ten pence a turd.'

'Eugh!' said Matt, flinching at the very thought.

'I think I'm gonna be sick,' said Ian.

The fact was, Matt needed the money by any means possible.

'Yeah, all right, you're on,' he said and went over to one of the kitchen drawers to get some doggie bags. 'Ah, show business, there's no business like it!'

14

Operation Haggis

'What's the sudden drive to raise money then?' said Ian later, wincing slightly as he burped up a little sausage surprise. 'You haven't got a gambling addiction, have you? I heard that a lot of kids have become addicted to those machines they have in the arcades.'

'Well . . .' said Matt. 'I am addicted to one machine.'

'I knew it,' said Ian, sitting up straight. 'What is it? The one-arm bandits or the gaming machines?'

'The grab machine where you try and pick up a stuffed toy,' laughed Matt. 'I'm desperate to win a Smurf!'

Ian tutted and shook his head. 'You got me! Fair enough, I walked into that, but come on, Matt, what are you saving up for?'

'I'm going to the Edinburgh Festival with Kitty and Neil and the rest of the gang. I'm going to get two whole weeks of gigs under my belt.'

'Er, hang on a sec,' said Ian, exchanging a look with Matt's mum. 'This is the first we've heard of it.'

'Yes, darling,' said Matt's mum, walking in from the kitchen holding a big fruit crumble. 'How are you going to get up there? Where are you going to stay? Who's supervising you? I mean, Scotland is a very dangerous place.'

'Particularly if you're a haggis!' said Matt with a laugh, reaching for his little black book. 'I'll be fine. Like I say, there's a whole gang of us going. There's safety in numbers. I'm a teenager now so—'

'Only just,' said Ian. 'We can't let you disappear off to what's as good as a foreign country and fend for yourself for fourteen days! What kind of parents would that make us?'

BEWARE OF THE HAGGIS!

MAN-EATING HAGGIS ON THE LOOSE!

DO NOT APPROACH!

'Good parents, that's what it would make you,' said Matt. He could feel his cheeks starting to burn as he got angry.

'No. I'm afraid not,' said his mum gently. 'Unless you've got an adult supervising you, you can forget all about it.'

'Couldn't one of you come up for a bit?' said Matt, starting to panic. Once again his dreams appeared to be slipping through his fingers.

'If I'm going on holiday for two weeks, the last place I want to spend it is blooming Scotland,' said Ian, batting the idea away dismissively. 'No offence to the Scots, but sorry, it's just not gonna happen!'

'Oh, come on,' snapped Matt angrily, jumping to his feet. 'What is your problem? I thought parents were supposed to support their kids? I thought you wanted me to make a success of my life!'

'Now hang on, darling ... !' said his mum, a little taken aback at the way the conversation had suddenly changed from playful banter to a full-blown argument.

'I'm going to the Edinburgh Festival and you're not going to stop me,' said Matt. He turned and marched out of the kitchen, slamming the door behind him, then he stomped up the stairs, making as much noise as he could, and into his bedroom.

It took him a good hour or so to calm down.

Although it was painful to admit, Ian and his mum had a point. How were they supposed to fend for themselves? They were, after all, just a bunch of kids.

He sent Kitty a one-word text. 'PROBLEM.'

Pretty much immediately his phone rang. He touched the little green phone sign and accepted her call.

'Hi, Kit,' he said. 'I've got a problem. My parents aren't keen on the trip.'

'Mine neither,' said Kitty. 'I've just had a flaming row with my dad. I was going to talk to you about it tomorrow. They've pretty much said I can't go unless we're supervised by an adult.'

'Snap,' said Matt, feeling a little better – the worst-case scenario was the others going and him being left behind. 'So come on then, manager, what's the plan? What are we going to do? Where can we get a friendly adult from?'

There was a heavy sigh from the other end of the phone line. 'I've been racking my brains, Matt. My parents won't do it.'

'Neither will mine.'

'Who else do we know? Someone from school? Maybe we could wangle it so it was a school trip or something . . .'

'In the holidays?' said Matt, shaking his head. 'Besides, what box does a trip to a comedy festival tick, as far as our education goes?'

'I don't know,' said Kitty. 'Music? Drama . . . ?'

Suddenly a light came on in Matt's brain. He remembered something that might just be the key to unlock their problem.

'I saw Mr Gillingham the other night with Miss Jolly,' he said, sitting bolt upright on his bed. 'What does she teach? Miss Jolly, what does she teach?'

'Drama!' said Kitty.

'Drama! Exactly! Mr G has always been really helpful. Now, if we can get him to get Miss Jolly interested in our show . . .'

'How would we do that?'

'By suggesting that the two of them come up to supervise us – it would be the perfect chance for them to get to know each other a little better!'

'Why don't we just contact Miss Jolly direct?' said Kitty.

'I don't know her. Besides, better for her to want to do it for more than one reason.'

'Wow, this is a new devious side to you I haven't seen before, Matt. That's really not a bad idea,' said Kitty.

'It's not only not a bad idea, it also happens to be our only idea,' said Matt.

'But drama's not the same as comedy ...' said Kitty, looking for holes in the plan. 'I mean, sometimes it's the opposite.'

'Listen, I know it's a long shot but surely it's worth a chance?'

'Yes, yes, sorry, you're right,' said Kitty.

'Great, but before you go, Kit, we need a code name for this plan, don't we?'

'Ha! Yes, we definitely need a code name.'

'OK, I'm calling it Operation Haggis. How about that?'

'Love it!' she said. 'Talk tomorrow!'

15

Brick Wall

It was just a few minutes after the school bell had sounded, but instead of leaving his English lesson, Matt hung back to talk to Mr Gillingham.

'Didn't you go up to the Edinburgh Festival when you were a student, sir?' said Matt.

'Yes, yes I did. How did you know about that?' said Mr G, looking up from his marking.

'You told me, sir.'

'Oh, did I? Great fun, but what about it? While I'd love to sit and chat, I've got to get this marking done ...'

Matt paused for a moment, pondering how

to phrase his proposition. 'I was thinking ...'
He faltered

'Always dangerous,' teased Mr G.

'About ... well, you know there are a few of us who are interested in going up to the festival this year?'

'Really?' said the teacher, looking up from his work. 'That's a great idea! You'll get so much out of it. You see, Matt, what Mr Pavey and all those Ofsted creeps don't understand is that education is about more than just exams and learning stuff by rote. Education is about experiencing new things. Oh, I think this trip is a great idea! I wish you the best of luck – I mean, it's years since I was up there but if there's anything I can do to help, let me know.' He opened another exercise book and raised his pen ready to mark it.

'Ah, well, there is something you might be able to help us with, sir,' said Matt tentatively. 'You see, we need an adult to take us – well, not to take us as such, but to er ... supervise us, so we were thinking—'

'Hang on, who's *we*?'

'Kitty Hope and me, we were thinking, how about making it a school trip?'

Mr Gillingham put down his pen again and sat forward. 'Well, I love the idea of a trip to the Fringe, but to qualify as a school trip it would have to be open to other members of the school. It's also not my department. You need to talk to—'

'Miss Jolly, sir,' Matt said with a cheeky smile.

Mr G narrowed his eyes and looked at Matt with an air of suspicion. 'Yes. Miss Jolly,' he said hesitantly.

'I don't have any lessons with her, sir. You and her seem to be, um, getting on very well, so I thought maybe you could plant the seed.'

'Hmmmmm,' said Mr G.

'Me and Kitty were thinking that a trip to Scotland for you and Miss Jolly might be something to look forward to . . .'

'Oh, you did, did you?' said Mr Gillingham a little testily. 'What is this? An episode of *First Dates*? When I need your advice on affairs of the heart, I'll ask, OK? Now if you'll excuse me, I've got some marking to do!'

With that he picked up his pen and carried on from where he'd left off. As Matt walked out, who should he bump into coming the other way but Miss Jolly.

'Hi, Miss Jolly,' he said cheerfully.

She nodded and walked on into the classroom.

'How'd it go?' said Kitty, who'd been waiting a discreet distance away down the corridor for any news.

'Not good,' said Matt. 'We're going to need to come up with another plan. I think Operation Haggis might be over before it's begun.'

16

Othello, Is It Me You're Looking For?

The following day Matt was wandering into school when he got a text through from Kitty.

'Come to noticeboard NOW,' it said.

'Noticeboard?' he muttered. 'Bit weird.' But he altered his course and strolled casually into the main school building and up the corridor to the area near the toilets where all the school announcements were pinned up on three noticeboards. One for sport, one for general announcements and one for school clubs.

There was a sizeable crowd gathered around the

school clubs one, and waiting at the fringes of it was Kitty Hope.

'What's all the fuss about?' said Matt nonchalantly.

'Best you take a look for yourself,' she said excitedly.

He shrugged and pushed at the scrum. 'Member of staff coming through,' he said in his gruffest voice, and the sea of kids miraculously parted, allowing him to march straight up to the front for a clear view of the board. Sure enough there was a roughly photocopied poster. The words printed on it sent a jolt of excitement through his young body.

ACTORS AND BACKSTAGE STAFF NEEDED FOR

Anglebrook Drama Society school trip to the Edinburgh Fringe Festival with William Shakespeare's
Othello.

AUDITIONS

Thursday and Friday lunch break, Drama Room, report to Miss Jolly.

'Wow!' he exclaimed. Then he felt a hand on his shoulder and he whipped round to see the smiling face of Mr Gillingham. 'So you had a word then, sir?' he said.

'Might have done,' said the teacher with an enigmatic smile.

'What's *Othello*?' asked Matt, joining Rob, Jamie and Ahmed on the steps of the science block at first break. They were all looking at one of Miss Jolly's posters sellotaped to the double doors.

'It's a play by William Shakespeare,' said Jamie.

'A rubbish poster, that,' said Rob, wagging his finger at it. 'I mean look at the typeface – my mum could have done better. I think I need to have a word with Miss Jolly and offer her my services.'

'I think Mr Gillingham's beaten you to it on that score,' said Ahmed with a cheeky grin.

Matt gave him a shove. 'Oi! What I told you is supposed to be top secret.'

'I've already signed up,' said Jamie.

'Oh yeah? Fancy yourself as a bit of a Benedict Cumber-Sprout, do you?' said Rob, giving Jamie a nudge.

BENEDICT CUMBER-SPROUT!

'I like Benedict's stuff for sure, but yeah, I'm interested in acting,' said Jamie defensively. 'Did a bit at my last school as a matter of fact. I'm even thinking, maybe it's something I could do for a living . . .' Then a distant look came into his eyes and he sighed. 'Problem is, I don't think my dad would be very pleased if I told him.'

The bell for end of break sounded and Rob and Ahmed peeled off towards the main building.

'Why not?' said Matt, hanging back with Jamie, the conversation suddenly taking an uncharacteristically serious turn.

'Oh, he doesn't have much time for stuff like that. Every time I bring it up he cracks jokes about "men in tights". No, he's made a lot of noises about me going to uni and doing what he calls a "proper" course – you know, English or Law or something . . .'

'Huh, talk about aiming low,' said Matt.

'Didn't you have any problems from your mum and dad about your stand-up thing?' said Jamie.

'I don't actually remember asking them,' said Matt. 'And Ian's my stepdad, not my real dad. I didn't ask them for permission, I just started doing it – or not doing it as the case may be.'

'Anyway, it's early days,' said Jamie. 'If I can get a good part in Miss Jolly's play and do well, then who knows, it might bring him round.'

'In my experience,' said Matt confidentially, 'I find

the only way to get adults to change their minds is to make them think it was their idea in the first place.'

'Ha!' laughed Jamie. 'Maybe I'll try that.' He paused. 'Dad says it's too tough to get on, that there's hundreds of out-of-work actors and who needs another one? He's got a point, I suppose.'

'Rubbish,' said Matt and he stopped walking and turned to face Jamie. 'What if Benedict Cumber-Sprout had taken your dad's advice? We never would have had *The Limitation Game*, *Showlock Humes* or *Dr Stranglehold*. No, someone's got to make it, so why can't it be you?'

Jamie nodded and smiled. 'Thanks, Matt, you're right,' he said. 'I could be the next Benny Cumber-Sprout!'

'You'll be in detention if you don't move your feet and get to lessons,' came a voice from behind them. It was the PE teacher Mr Avery. 'Now hop it!'

They both looked at each other, laughed, then tucked one leg up and literally hopped to their next lesson.

'It's a play about rivalry and jealousy, isn't that right, sir?' said Kitty. She and Matt had arranged to meet Mr Gillingham after school to discuss the Edinburgh trip.

'That's right, Kitty. Othello is an African general who becomes insanely jealous and tries to murder his great love Desdemona, but ends up killing his right-hand man instead and in the end himself. A lesson there for all of us. It's a great *English* play! And as such, of course, it's very important that I accompany Miss Jolly on the trip.'

'Hmmm, doesn't sound like a barrel of laughs, sir,' said Matt. 'When I said I was up for taking a show to the festival, I was talking about a stand-up comedy show, not some old play ...'

'It's the only way it can work, Matt. I told you, for it to qualify as a school trip it has to be open to everyone.'

'But if we're up there anyway ...?' said Kitty, blinking hopefully up at Mr Gillingham through her spectacles.

Mr Gillingham nodded. 'Yes, well, if you're in Edinburgh with the school, doing a proper literary piece, then it doesn't seem to me beyond the bounds of possibility that you might put on a stand-up show in your spare time in the same venue . . .' he said with a conspiratorial sideways glance.

'Yes!' said Matt, jumping up and punching the air in triumph. 'The haggis has landed!' Then he turned to Kitty and high-fived her.

'Hang on!' said Mr Gillingham, making a calming

motion with his hand. 'Before you get too excited, you're not necessarily in the play yet. You may be Matt Millz, the famous stand-up comic, but you've got to pass the audition like everyone else.'

Matt nodded. 'Fair enough,' he said. 'Bring it on!'

17

Audition Time Again

'How was it?' said Matt to Neil Trottman as he walked out of the drama room and into the waiting area. It was the second day of the auditions and Miss Jolly was putting them through their paces in small groups.

'Er . . . well, it seemed to go OK. She just got me to read a few bits of the play, with some of the others – Ayeesha, Janine and Alex . . .'

'He was brilliant,' said Alex, pushing through the door just a few moments behind Neil. Her face was flushed red and there were small beads of sweat on her brow. 'Phew! I'm glad that's over!' she said, flopping down on one of the chairs.

'You weren't so bad yourself!' said Neil.

'Hmm, looks like they may have found their Othello and Desdemona,' said Jamie who was also in Matt's group.

'Oh, I shouldn't think so,' said Alex, fanning her face with a book. 'It didn't go that well – I mean it's impossible to tell, isn't it, Neil?' she said, looking over at the younger boy.

'Yeah, Miss J doesn't give much away,' said Neil.

At that point the lady in question popped her head round the door. 'Right,' she said, studying a clipboard. 'Jamie Castle, Sally Rainham, Sean Ransford, Debbie Smith and Matt Mills please,' she said, looking at Matt and smiling, which to Matt felt like a good sign.

'Fingers crossed then,' muttered Matt to Alex.

'Oh, you'll be fine – you're a natural performer,' she said admiringly. 'You'll walk it!'

They sat in a semicircle as Miss Jolly explained how the audition would work.

'So, all I want you to do is read a couple of the parts as best you can. Any questions?'

Matt's hand shot up as if to ask a question. 'Yes, miss, just to say I forgot to bring my leotard!'

The rest of the group sniggered, although Jamie seemed completely focused on the job in hand.

'Leotards will not be necessary, Matt,' said Miss Jolly, rolling her eyes. 'And I'd appreciate it if you took this rather more seriously. You may think that because you've been on telly that you're going to walk into one of the best parts – but I'm afraid I'll be judging you solely on how you do today.'

Jamie Castle nodded in agreement. Matt felt suitably chastised, and in fact a bit silly. Suddenly it dawned on him that getting a part in the play and therefore being able to go on the Edinburgh trip wasn't necessarily a done deal. He needed to pass this silly audition first. He looked across at Jamie who was deep in thought, flicking through his own copy of the play and suddenly wished he'd done a bit of preparation.

'You're the last lot and I have to tell you the main part, the part of Othello, has already gone,' said Miss

Jolly. 'I haven't told him yet, but I've seen someone who is really going to be great in the role. Right then, let's get going.' She started to hand out photocopied sheets.

'It's OK, miss,' said Jamie, holding up his well-thumbed paperback of *Othello*. 'I've got my own copy.'

Matt rolled his eyes – it seemed Jamie was taking this audition very seriously indeed.

'OK, in that case, Jamie, as you seem to be familiar with the script, do you want to go first?'

Jamie jumped up. 'Yes, miss. I'd love to,' he said.

'Since you've clearly been studying it, is there a particular speech you'd like to try?' she said.

'Oh well, there is one bit that I've actually learned . . .'

Matt groaned. 'What a swot,' he thought to himself. There was no way he could compete with that.

Miss Jolly looked surprised. 'Well, I must say that's above and beyond the call of duty. But very much appreciated. In your own time then, off you go!'

Jamie rose to his feet and stepped forward into the semicircle formed by the other children's chairs, then he turned to face the rest of the auditionees. He looked at the floor as if deep in thought. When he looked back up to face them, a change had come across him.

"'I follow him to serve my turn upon him:'" he intoned.

"'We cannot all be masters, nor all masters
Cannot be truly follow'd. You shall mark
Many a duteous and knee-crooking knave . . .'"

Matt and the rest of the gang watched spellbound as Jamie delivered the lines. It was like Jamie had become another person.

It was weird; when Matt had looked at Shakespeare's words before, he'd never really understood what this old guy from way back was on about with all those 'thy's and 'thee's. It was like a foreign language. But in Jamie's hands, suddenly the text came alive, and although Matt didn't necessarily understand all the individual words, the meaning of them was crystal clear. He couldn't help but join the others in a spontaneous round of applause as Jamie finished.

Miss Jolly was straight up on her feet and strode across to congratulate him.

'I think we've found our Iago,' she said, shaking him enthusiastically by the hand. 'That was really great, Jamie. I don't know what your plans are for GCSEs – I guess it's a bit early to have given it much thought – but I'd like you to think about opting for Drama.'

'I'd really like that,' said Jamie, beaming.

'So that doesn't leave many of the big parts for the rest of you,' said Miss Jolly, turning to the group.

One by one they stood up and read from Miss Jolly's sheets. Some of them were pretty terrible, some of them so-so, but none of them came near to Jamie. Last of all, it was Matt's turn.

'Matt – perhaps you could read the part of Roderigo …'

'Hmmmm …' huffed Matt. He was starting to feel really out of his comfort zone. He took the sheet from Miss Jolly and stood in the middle of the semicircle. He looked at the script, cleared his throat and launched himself into it.

'"Tush!"' he exclaimed.

Miss Jolly interrupted him straight away. 'Er, that's pronounced *tush*, like *whoosh*!' she said

'Right, OK,' said Matt. 'I'll be honest – it's not a word I use a lot.' There were a few sniggers from the other kids in the semicircle.

'It's a mild expletive,' said Miss Jolly. 'A bit like damn, or what the heck.'

'Oh, thanks,' said Matt with a smile. 'I must remember that for next time I get in a spot of bother. Oh, tush! I've forgotten to bring my homework to school! Or, oh, tush! the dog's been sick on the carpet!'

'Ahem,' interjected Miss Jolly, a little annoyed. 'This is all very amusing, Matt, but can we try to stick to the script? You're not auditioning for *The T Factor* now, thank you very much.'

'Sorry, miss,' said Matt with a sly wink to Jamie, who grinned back.

'Right, from the top then,' said Miss Jolly.

'"Tush! Never tell me; I take it much unkindly ..." Sorry, Miss Jolly, but that must be a misprint,' he said, looking up from the page at his teacher. 'It says "I take it much unkindly". Shouldn't that be "That's a bit much, a bit unkind?" Or something . . .' Matt petered out as he saw how annoyed Miss Jolly was starting to get at his interruptions.

'It was written in the sixteenth century,' she

snapped. 'Sorry, Matt, but it's written how they spoke back then, so please, *just stick to the script*,' she said, looking at her watch.

'Whatevs,' said Matt, and launched into the speech once again. '"That thou, Iago, who hast had my purse—"' He stopped and burst out laughing. 'A purse! Ha ha! What self-respecting bloke carries a purse? I s'pose he keeps it in his handbag, does he?' The whole group erupted in laughter. Even Jamie was cracking up.

'Got a point,' said one of the other kids.

That was the last straw for Miss Jolly. 'Right! That's it! Thank you, Matt, I'll let you know,' she said, gathering up the sheets and stacking the chairs.

'But . . . I didn't do the whole thing!' protested Matt.

'No, but you did enough. Thank you and there'll be a full list of who's got what parts on the noticeboard at the end of play today.'

'I have got a part though, haven't I, miss?' said Matt, starting to panic.

'Like I say, there'll be a full list on the noticeboard this afternoon,' she said, pulling on her jacket and heading for the door.

Matt looked at Jamie, who shrugged. If he hadn't got a part in the play, his trip to Edinburgh was off, and judging from Miss Jolly's attitude it looked very much like he hadn't.

There was only one word to explain how he felt right at that moment.

'Tush!' said Matt.

18
No Certainties

Matt had been kept late after maths, again, while Miss Stake had gone through the finer points of the square root, so by the time he got to the lobby there was a large crowd round the noticeboard jostling to get a look at who'd been chosen for the drama society's Edinburgh trip. As Matt tried to push through, a familiar face came the other way from deep within the throng. It was Neil Trottman, and he was looking slightly stunned.

'I don't believe it,' he said, blinking and shaking his head.

'What?' said Matt urgently. 'Did you get a part?'

'I didn't just get a part,' said Neil. 'I got *the* part – she's cast me as Othello!'

'Wow!' exclaimed Matt. 'Way to go! Nice one! Ha ha!' he said, clapping Neil on the back. 'You didn't by any chance see my name on the list, did you?' he said nervously, trying to look over the heads of the crowd to get a look at the board.

'No, I didn't see your name,' said Neil, then clocked the worried look on Matt's face. 'I mean, I wasn't looking for your name, I was looking for mine, so ... I'm sure you would have got a part though, wouldn't you?'

That was just it, there was no certainty. The next person to emerge from the throng was Jamie C, looking particularly pleased with himself.

'Did you see my name?' said Matt.

'Er ... look, it's probably best if you check it out yourself, Matt,' said Jamie awkwardly.

Matt frowned and pushed hard at the back of the crowd. He got to the front eventually, but not without ruffling a few feathers.

'Oi! Watch who you're pushing!'

'Hey! We're all trying to see it, mate!'

As he got closer to the front he pulled someone's shoulder to get in front of them and the person attached to the shoulder turned round sharply.

'Watch it, you—!' It was Rob. 'Oh. Hi, Matt.'

'Well?' said Matt. 'Did you get a part?'

'Small one, yeah. Cassio,' said Rob with a nod. 'It's all I wanted really. I'm only going for the fun – I'm not that interested in acting.'

'What about me? Am I on the list?'

'Be my guest,' said Rob and gave Matt his place in front of the noticeboard.

Matt quickly scanned the list – there was no sign of his name. Tush and double tush!

'I don't believe it.' he said. 'This was my idea! I can't believe everyone's going up except me.'

Maybe he'd had his life's worth of luck that time at the Apollo, at *The T Factor*. Maybe from now on this was how it was going to be. Maybe he'd never get the break he was looking for and eventually he'd give up on the idea of a life as a stand-up and settle for a job in estate agenting like his stepdad Ian.

'What's the news?' said Kitty, running up to join him as he peeled away from the board.

'She's left me off the—' said Matt.

'The what?' said a voice from a few yards away. Matt spun round to see Miss Jolly and Mr Gillingham.

'Nothing,' said Matt, with a lump in his throat.

'You're right, Matt. I have left you off the list, simply because I didn't think you were taking the play seriously enough. There's a surprising amount of talent in this little school,' the drama teacher said, looking at Mr Gillingham, who nodded.

'But Paul – I mean *Mr Gillingham* here – has explained to me about your plan to do a stand-up show so I'm going to give you the benefit of the doubt.'

By now the crowd gathered round the noticeboard had all turned and were hanging on Miss Jolly's every word. 'There is a small part for you,' she said, taking down the original list and pinning up a new one. 'It's the part of the clown, and you can understudy Jamie for the part of Iago, which means you'll have to learn it.'

Jamie turned to Matt and patted him gently on the back. Matt was so unbelievably pleased that he lunged at Miss Jolly, flung his arms around her and gave her a big hug.

'Thanks, miss,' he gushed. 'I promise I won't let you down.' Then he turned to the crowd and punched the air. 'We're going to Edinburgh! Yay!'

And the crowd all cheered.

CAST LIST

OTHELLO - Neil Trottman

IAGO - Jamie Castle

DESDEMONA - Alex Williams

CASSIO - Rob Brown

EMILIA - Kitty Hope

BIANCA AND DOGE OF VENICE -
Ayeesha Phillips

BRABANTIO AND MONTANO -
Alan Thorpe

RODERIGO - Stanley Baker

LODOVICA - Frederica Hall

CLOWN - Matthew Mills

MAKE UP & WARDROBE - Magda Avery

SOUND & LIGHTS - Ahmed Chalabi

19
Poster Boy

'How'd you get on at the auditions?' said Ian, flinging his briefcase on to the sofa as he walked into the front room that evening after work.

'I got the part of the clown,' said Matt brightly.

'Figures,' said Ian.

'Yeah, I hate clowns and I've only got three lines.'

'Hmmm, that's a long way to go for three lines,' said Ian.

'The bad news is I've got to learn the part of Iago too – I'm understudy to Jamie Castle.'

'Like stepfather like stepson,' said Ian, shaking his head. 'Seems like it's a family tradition for us to play second fiddle to the Castles. I tell you, that bloke is really winding me up,' said Ian, wandering into the kitchen and making a beeline for the fridge. He unclipped a can of Coke, popped the ring pull and took a long slug.

'Oh, that tastes good,' he said, flopping back into his favourite armchair. 'All he's interested in is flaming paperwork. I tell you, if he carries on like this I'm going to have to seriously think about getting a job elsewhere. He's got this really high-handed manner about him too – sorry, Matt, I know Jamie's your friend, but his dad treats me like I'm a complete imbecile.'

'Well, he's got a point,' laughed Matt and ducked as Ian flung a cushion at him.

Knowing he had the promise of a run of back-to-back gigs meant that Matt's time at school was a lot more bearable. He could now put up with the boredom of double physics and the petty school rules because he had something to look forward to. It was true that the Edinburgh Festival was a good three months away, but at least he now had something to work towards.

Miss Jolly gave them a couple of weeks to familiarise themselves with the plot and lines, then rehearsals started every Thursday after school. As the date got closer they were more regular, often during lunch breaks and at weekends. Aware that they only had an hour slot, Miss Jolly had made some big cuts to the plot. 'We're not trying to do the whole Royal Shakespeare thing,' she'd explained. 'It's more we're trying to give a flavour of what this story is about – about power, jealousy and rage.'

Matt had to admit that Neil and Jamie were really knocking it out of the park with their parts. Neil had the idea fairly early on to turn one of Othello's speeches into a rap – he'd even come up with a backing track, and so far it was easily the highlight of the play.

Everyone was really impressed with Jamie Castle

too. As Iago, Othello's treacherous assistant, it wasn't like he was delivering lines, it was if he actually became the character of Iago. Even Matt couldn't take his eyes off him.

Alex was doing a good job as Othello's wife Desdemona – she'd decided to use the voice of Haley Wallaby, the daytime TV presenter – although Matt found himself feeling oddly jealous when Neil and her had to get close. Miss Jolly had cut the bit where they were supposed to kiss – much to everyone's relief.

Matt knew the fact that he had to learn the huge part of Iago, as well as the few lines that belonged to the clown, was Miss Jolly's way of testing him. This time he was determined not to let her or Mr Gillingham down and he ran through them whenever he could by recording them on his smartphone and playing them back after he'd repeated them. He found the rehearsals for the play pretty boring – mainly because he had so little to do. 'It's such a small part,' he had protested at an early rehearsal.

'There are no small parts, Matt,' Miss Jolly riposted. 'Just small actors.'

'Ouch,' said Rob.

'Listen, Matt, if you can't be bothered to rehearse properly – and that means keeping quiet while the others are running through their parts, then perhaps you'd be better off not being in the play at all,' she snapped during one rehearsal after he'd cracked a joke.

'The thing is, there aren't many jokes in Shakespeare, are there, miss?' said Matt.

'Othello is a tragedy,' replied Miss Jolly testily.

'You're telling me, miss,' said Matt, to a big laugh from the rest of the cast.

'These texts are over five hundred years old—' she continued.

'Yeah, and it shows,' said Matt. 'The whole thing could do with an update. How come Iago doesn't just phone Cassio, instead of having to track him down to that bridge? No, I think there's huge room for improvement.'

'That's a gag, right?' said Rob, leaning in and laughing.

'Huh?' said Matt.

'That's a routine you're working on, about modernising Shakespeare?'

'It is now,' said Matt, his hand delving into his pocket for his little black book.

'Actually, there are a *lot* of jokes in Shakespeare,' Miss Jolly said. 'In fact, there's a little job for you, to keep you busy. Tonight I want you to write me a list of William Shakespeare's best jokes.'

'Oh, miss,' groaned Matt.

'Yes, that'll teach you to horse around in my rehearsals.'

That night Matt typed 'Shakespeare jokes' into Google and waited to see what it came up with.

SHAKESPEARE JOKES

I would challenge you
to a battle of wits, but
I see you are unarmed.
(*Much Ado About Nothing*)

Your brain is as dry as the remainder
biscuit after voyage. (*As You Like It*)

Many a good hanging prevents a bad
marriage. (*Twelfth Night*)

The tautness of his face sours ripe grapes.
(*Coriolanus*)

He didn't think any of them were particularly
funny. 'I get that Shakespeare was a pretty successful
writer of plays but I can't see him lasting five minutes
at the Comedy Store!' he thought to himself.

In the meantime Kitty had started planning the

show that really mattered to Matt – the stand-up show. She'd had a word with Miss Jolly and Mr Gillingham and they'd agreed it would take place at half past four in the afternoon, just half an hour after the school play finished up.

'We need another act,' she told Matt. She explained that while he was down to do twenty minutes – which would be the most he'd ever done in one go – Alex could really only stretch to ten minutes and Neil was happy to do ten, so that meant that they were fifteen to twenty minutes short of a full hour-long show.

'How about Bobby?' said Matt.

Kitty shrugged. 'No, I think it needs to be someone of our age, and preferably someone who's in the play already so we don't have to go through the whole "unsupervised" business.'

'Rob?' said Matt, but even as he said it he knew that Rob would never agree to trying stand-up again. The last and only time he'd attempted it as a double act with Matt at the school talent show,

Rob had been physically sick with nerves and once on stage had frozen in fear, leaving Matt to take over.

'I don't think so, do you?' said Kitty, her hands on her hips. 'No, there'll be someone, and we don't need their name right now – but we'll need it by early June because that's when we have to register for the Fringe.'

'What do you think we should call it?' said Matt.

'Well, the competition for an audience is going to be really tough up there so we should play on any advantage we can lay our hands on,' she said.

'Meaning?' asked Matt.

'I think we should call it *Matt Millz and Friends*, don't you?' she said.

He liked the sound of that!

Kitty retrieved a sheet of A3 paper from her satchel and flopped it on to the desk in front of them. It had some type and rough caricatures of Matt, Neil and Alex, and the outline of a fourth person with a big question mark where their face would be.

"'Fresh from hit TV show *The T Factor* . . .'" Matt smiled. Fresh? It was over a year ago! "'Matt Millz – the youngest stand-up comic ever to raise the roof at the Hammersmith Apollo.'"

Hmm, it didn't mention the fact that he'd bottled it the second time.

'"Featuring up-and-coming impressionist ..."
Up-and-coming? She's done less gigs than I have!'
said Matt with a chuckle.

'We've got to be a little economical with the truth
if we're going to stand any chance of selling it,'
said Kitty.

'"Rapper and body-popper Neil Trottman ... and
TBA." Who's TBA?' said Matt.

'To Be Arranged,' said Kitty, taking the poster
back from him. 'For the time being we'll just leave a
gap for the fourth name.'

'So you're happy with it then?' said Kitty.
'The poster?'

'Oh yes,' said Matt. Seeing it written down made
it seem all the more real. 'Very, very happy with it.'

'Great! To *Matt Millz and Friends*!' she said.

20

The Fourth Act

'Hi, Matt, It's Kitty!'

'I know, your name comes up on my phone when you call me,' replied Matt.

'Listen, I think I've found our fourth act,' she said excitedly.

'Yeah?' said Matt, more than a little intrigued.

'Yes, I'm quite excited actually. He's really talented. I've even signed him up to the agency,' she gushed.

'Oh yeah, that's good ...' he said, trying to match her excitement but failing miserably, feeling a stab of jealousy in his gut. 'How did you find him?'

'Well, he found me,' said Kitty. 'And there's no

problem with him joining us as he's going to be in Edinburgh anyway – he's in the school play!'

'What are you talking about, Kit?' said Matt, racking his brains to try and come up with a possible name. 'Come on, spill the beans? Who is this mystery comic?'

'Well, you know him actually – of course. It's been staring us in the face all along. It's Jamie Castle!'

'Sorry, did you say Jamie Castle?' said Matt, completely taken aback.

'Yes, that's right. Jamie . . .'

'That's weird, Jamie's never mentioned anything about wanting to be a comic. In fact, he told me once he could never do it. I mean, he's a great actor, yes, but . . .'

'Well, he's got loads of great ideas for routines,' said Matt's pint-sized manager. 'And from what I've seen, he's really funny,' she added, almost squealing with delight.

'Hang on, hang on . . . !' said Matt. 'How? When? When exactly did you see Jamie being funny?'

'Oh, well, he approached me this morning at break.'

Matt blinked and shook his head momentarily disorientated. 'He approached you? That's really odd because I saw Jamie then and he didn't mention—'

'Well, I guess he feels slightly awkward, what with you being the number-one comic in the school.'

'Huh, maybe . . .' puzzled Matt.

'Anyway, he came to the DMC at lunchtime and ran a couple of routines, and I won't lie, I was blown away,' she said. 'Great gags and a really unusual style too.'

Matt was now contorting inside with jealousy. 'Is he really that good, Kit?' he asked. 'I mean, I don't want to pour cold water on your idea, and believe me it would be great to nail down that fourth act, but we both know it takes stage time to become a stand-up – I mean, look at me, look how much work I've put in and I'm not . . .'

'Someone sounds a bit jealous,' said Kitty, disappointed at Matt's lack of enthusiasm.

'Well, I mean you've got to admit it's a bit odd,' said Matt.

'Jamie says he did some gigs in South Africa when he was over there and attended a few stand-up workshops, so—'

'He never mentioned that to me,' said Matt.

'Look, you're just going to have to trust me, aren't you, Matt,' said Kitty a little coldly. 'That is, unless you're not happy for Jamie to be on the bill?'

'No, no, I'm not saying that,' said Matt, backtracking. 'Listen, Kit. If you think he's up to it, that's fine by me – I'm just a little surprised, that's all.'

'Well, stranger things have happened and yes, I am happy he's up to it, as you put it – more than happy. I think he could be a big star for the future.'

'Great, then stick him on the poster.' said Matt, but as he hung up he was more than a little confused.

Jamie was a great actor, no doubt about it – he'd proved that in the auditions and then in the rehearsals for *Othello* – but funny? He had a good sense of humour, sure, and was fun to be with – sort of – but a stand-up comic? Matt shook his head and tried to think of a time when Jamie had made him, or anyone else for that matter, laugh. No, Jamie was someone who laughed along with gags, not someone who made them up. What's more, he hadn't mentioned to Matt that he was interested in becoming a stand-up. It seemed a bit weird, didn't it? After all, Matt hung out with Jamie most days.

No, something about Jamie's sudden comic abilities didn't smell quite right.

'I suppose I should have checked with you before talking to Kitty,' said Jamie the next day when Matt gently cornered him in the playground about his new-found desire to become a stand-up comic.

'I was a bit surprised,' said Matt. 'It's just that when we talked about it at your house, you said you'd be too scared to try it and you certainly didn't mention that you were working on an act.'

'Er, didn't I?' said Jamie defensively. 'I think we did talk about stand-up when we first met, didn't we?'

'Yes, we talked about it, about who we liked,' said Matt, 'but you never said you wanted to be one or that you had an act or you'd been to these stand-up workshops back in South Africa.'

Jamie shifted uneasily; this was a slightly awkward conversation for both of them, but Matt felt it had to be brought out into the open.

'Well, maybe I . . . maybe I was a bit nervous and wasn't thinking straight. You know, I'd never met you properly before, I'd only ever seen you on TV, so I was a bit star-struck . . .'

'Star-struck? Ha! OK! If you say so,' said Matt.

'You're not upset, are you?' said Jamie. 'I mean, I don't want to tread on your toes, so if you'd rather I didn't do it or looked for another agent . . .'

'No, no, I mean I don't have any control over who Kitty signs up – she's her own girl. She's a tough crowd too, so I know she wouldn't be interested in you unless she thought you had talent. Like I say, it was just a bit of a surprise, that's all,' said Matt, satisfied for the time being with Jamie's explanation. 'No, no, actually it's good news. It'll be nice to have someone who's as interested in the business as I am.' He thrust his hand out and shook Jamie's hand. 'Welcome to the Kitty Hope Comedy Agency. I can't wait to see your act!'

21

A Rich Man's World

With just over six weeks to go before the Edinburgh trip, Matt and Kitty went back to the routine they'd established for his *T Factor* audition. Every break he'd meet her in the DMC and run his routines. She'd time him and give him notes. It wasn't the same as doing it in front of an audience but it did help build his confidence and the more he ran the gags the more he found ways to get to the punchline more quickly or develop other little diversions along the way.

He had a lot of stuff, a lot of ideas, and his main problem was deciding which to pick to develop and which to put to one side for the future.

'That's great, Matt!' said Kitty as he finished a practice run. 'It's really beginning to shape up – there's a good twenty there!'

'Cheers, Kit,' said Matt, flopping into a chair. 'Listen, how's Jamie's act coming along? I don't see you doing the same workout with him?'

'It's weird,' said Kitty. 'He doesn't want to practise and he's adamant about it. He says he's worked out what he wants to do, so there's no need.'

'That's pretty confident for someone who's never done any gigs,' said Matt.

'Yes, maybe even a bit silly, but like I said, what he told me was really funny – and, well, polished, and I can't exactly force him to rehearse, can I?'

'Whenever I ask him about it he changes the subject. Like he doesn't want me to know what he's up to, which is weird,' said Matt.

'He's basically quite shy, I think,' said Kitty.

Although Matt's act was coming together nicely, cash flow was still a problem. Would they actually be able to put on their show? Matt didn't know, but then Mr Gillingham caught up with him and Rob one evening as they finished their rehearsal.

'How's the fundraising going?' he asked, a big grin on his face.

'Not too good, I'm afraid,' said Matt.

'Nor me,' said Rob.

'Well, I've got a little bit of good news for you both,' he said. 'A local businessman has offered to sponsor the whole trip!'

'Sponsor?' said Matt.

'Yes, he's offering to pay all the costs apart from the travel. Which leaves each student with a bill of just forty-five pounds! Not bad, eh?' he said with a chuckle.

'Yay!' said Matt

'Who's the businessman, sir?' said Rob.

'Well, he's not just a businessman.' He hesitated, a little reluctant to spill the beans on the identity of their mystery saviour. 'OK, this is not for general dissemination around school – the businessman is

Jamie Castle's dad.'

'Wow! That's pretty generous,' said Rob.

'Yes, the only downside is that we have to have an inflatable house outside the venue advertising his business, but I can live with that. Like I say, lads, mum's the word,' said Mr G conspiratorially.

'Your boss is paying for the entire trip,' said Matt to Ian as he walked in the front door just forty minutes later.

'Eh?' said Ian, flinging his briefcase on to the sofa and striding towards the fridge for a cold drink.

'Jamie's dad is sponsoring our Edinburgh trip!'

'That pain in the—'

'Dinner's ready,' shrilled Mum, meeting him halfway holding a big steaming saucepan. 'And it's your favourite. Sausage surprise!'

It was all Matt and Ian could do to stop themselves from groaning.

22

The Tartan Express

'Right! All aboard the Tartan Express!' called Mr Gillingham as he manhandled suitcases on to the roof rack of the school minibus.

'Say goodbye to your parents, kids,' said Miss Jolly. 'Now has everyone got everything?'

'Too bad if they haven't,' muttered Mr G under his breath as he climbed into the driver's seat.

Matt walked over to say goodbye to his mum and Ian. Mrs Mills grabbed him and pulled him towards her and gave him a semi-asphyxiating hug.

'Be careful,' she said.

'It's only Scotland, Jenny,' said Ian, taking the next

hug. 'Have a great time! We're hoping to come up for the last weekend so we'll see you then, and any problems, we're just on the end of the phone.'

'Call me when you get there,' added his mum.

There were fourteen of them in all – twelve kids and Mr G and Miss Jolly – so it was all a bit of a crush, but everyone was in an excitable mood as their Scottish adventure finally got under way.

'Hang on,' said Rob. 'Where's Jamie?'

'Ah, well, Master Castle is making his own way up. Seems his dad has organised his transport. For some reason his mum and dad didn't like the idea of him stuck on a motorway in an overcrowded minibus for twelve hours so he's flying!'

'Wow! Flying!' said Matt.

'Classic Jamie,' nodded Ahmed.

'Must be made of money,' said Rob.

'I think they are actually, Rob,' said Mr G.

'Don't knock it,' said Miss Jolly. 'It's thanks to Mr Castle that we're going at all.'

'How's that, miss?' asked Ahmed.

'He's the local businessman who's sponsoring the show,' she said, and handed him a leaflet.

'First time I've seen an advert for *Othello* with Iago as the main character – but there we are,' said Mr Gillingham, exchanging a knowing look with Miss Jolly. 'Commerce is the great civiliser. I can't remember who said that, but it's very apt.'

'So if Jamie wants to fly up or be driven in a Rolls-Royce that's fine by me!' said Miss Jolly.

Mr G beeped the horn a couple of times as they drove down the school drive, out on to the main road and towards their new adventure.

They got as far as the Hangar Lane gyratory system on the outskirts of west London when there was a loud pop from under the bonnet. Suddenly the minibus filled with smoke and Mr G pulled on to the nearest pavement.

'Everyone out!' he barked. Everyone filed out and stood coughing and spluttering on the side of the road as Mr G had a look under the bonnet.

'Well, this is a good start,' he said, shaking his head as he called the roadside rescue service. Miss Jolly took the kids off to a nearby cafe and they all had a drink and a packet of crisps and used the loo.

When they got back the minibus was being loaded on to a pickup truck and Mr Gillingham was sitting at the wheel of a brand-new Mercedes 'splitter' bus.

'Where did you steal this?' asked Miss Jolly, hurrying the kids on to the bus to take up their new seats.

'The big end had gone,' he said to Miss Jolly. 'The engine was completely knackered. The insurance company substituted it with this from a local garage. Haha!'

'That was quick,' said Miss Jolly, joining him at the front.

'Yeah, well, I stressed there were kids involved and how we had a long journey ahead of us, but result, eh?'

'Too right, sir,' piped up Matt from the back.

'Yeah! Jamie Castle can stick his plane. We've got a DVD player,' said Ahmed, fiddling with the TV screen that hung between the front and back seats. 'And DVDs too,' he said, opening an overhead locker to reveal a rack of about twenty DVDs.

'Have a great trip,' said the driver of the pickup truck in a broad Scottish accent. 'An' gi' me regards to the auld country!'

They made good progress in the new vehicle and although they spent most of their time with their eyes glued to the TV, they were aware of the scenery changing as they headed north.

It was almost midnight when they arrived in

Edinburgh. The streets were still crammed with people as crowds of festival-goers milled about intent on having fun.

'This is Princes Street,' said Mr Gillingham as they got on to what looked like the main drag. 'And that up there –' he pointed to the right where Matt could see high above them on a huge rocky outcrop the silhouette of a castle – 'is Edinburgh Castle!'

The kids all exclaimed with excitement. Although just moments before most of them had been fast asleep, they were now all wide awake and buzzing with the excitement of what lay before them.

'Oh, hang on,' said Mr Gillingham. 'Looking at the satnav we've got a bit further to go yet. The hostel must be a little way out of the town centre.

A 'little way out' was something of an understatement.

'Blimey, if we were any further out we'd be in Aberdeen,' joked Miss Jolly as the minibus pulled up at a farmhouse at the end of a long country lane about an hour from the city centre.

An old lady stood at the door with what looked like an old-fashioned lantern held aloft.

'You must be the young folk from Kent,' she said, a welcoming grin spreading across her face. 'I'm Mrs Irene McEwan and welcome to Arbroath Farm!'

Behind Mrs McEwan stood a familiar face in dressing gown and pyjamas – it was Jamie Castle.

23

Zombie Leisure Centre

They were in fairly basic mini-dormitories and divided up into girls and boys. There were bunk beds and a sink at one end, while down the corridor were the washrooms and showers. Mrs McEwan brought them all round a choice of soup or a sandwich, and despite the late hour Mr Gillingham told them they were allowed forty minutes before they had to turn in.

While the others mucked about, Matt sat on his bunk going through his set list for the following day. He was excited but also very, very nervous. He kept looking at the list thinking, 'Maybe if I moved that bit there and that bit there . . .' But really he had no idea how any of it was going to go as he'd tried out so little of it in front of an audience.

The next morning they were woken by Mrs McEwan rattling a wooden spoon in a tin bucket. When he first opened his eyes Matt had absolutely no clue where he was. Then within a matter of seconds he put two and two together and remembered it was the first day of their Edinburgh adventure and they had a show to do. Not just one show, either – two! And it was the second one he was most interested in. *Matt Millz and Friends*.

After a delicious, but not terribly healthy, traditional Scottish breakfast of bacon, egg, sausages, black pudding, baked beans and something called a 'tattie scone' (a sort of fried bread) they piled back into the splitter bus. Miss Jolly was eager to get into the city and check out the venue. She had twelve children under fourteen to wrangle, scenery to put up, lights and sound to check out, and despite the fact that the dress rehearsal had gone well, like most of the team she was a bag of nerves. The difference between her and the cast was that she had to keep her nerves hidden.

Matt still had no clue what Jamie's act consisted of.

'So what are you doing in your set?' he asked him as they trundled through the city in the minibus.

'Oh well, you know, fifteen minutes ...' said Jamie vaguely.

'No, I mean, what kind of stuff? One-liners? Routines? Shaggy-dog stories, surreal stuff, audience banter ...'

'Well, I'd rather not talk about it,' said Jamie. 'You'll see soon enough.'

'It's just that it would be good to know if there's any stuff we overlap on,' said Matt, trying a different tack.

'Well,' said Jamie, giving it some thought. 'How about you tell me what's in your set and I'll tell you if I'm doing anything similar?'

'I have to say, Jamie, you're being very secretive.

We've got our first show tonight and no one's even seen your act!'

'Kitty's seen it,' said Jamie, finally turning to face Matt. 'I dunno, I'm shy just talking to you one on one, but I'm hoping once I get out there in front of an audience I'll be OK, just like with my acting, I s'pose.'

'Phew,' said Matt, giving up any hope of a preview. 'Well, all I can say is I can't wait to to see it!'

'I really hope you like it, Matt. I'm looking forward to seeing your act too.'

'It should be down here, Paul! I mean, Mr Gillingham,' said Miss Jolly as the bus lurched down a cobbled street in the sheeting rain.

'I've never seen rain like this. It's like a monsoon,' he said.

'A Monsoon?' said Magda, screwing her face up. 'I don't know what branch of Monsoon you're using, but it must have a plumbing problem.'

'Not the shop Monsoon,' said Mr G, rolling his

eyes and shaking his head. 'Somebody tell Ms Avery what a monsoon is.'

'It's another word for a rainy season – they have one in India, don't they, sir?' said one of the younger kids.

'That is correct,' said Mr G, fiddling with the satnav. 'Are you sure this is the right place, Steph? We're still a long way out of the city centre.'

The kids sniggered at finding out Miss Jolly's first name.

'That's what it says on the letter,' said Miss Jolly. 'Look, there's a sign – *Splashes Leisure Centre*. That's it!'

'Hang on, we're playing a leisure centre?' droned Ahmed from the back seat.

'Yeah, I hope I'm in the shallow end,' joked Matt, which got a good laugh and sent him reaching into his jacket pocket for his little black book.

'All sorts of places are turned into venues during the festival, Ahmed,' called out Kitty Hope from up front.

'When we came here, all those years ago, we did our show in a church,' chuckled Mr Gillingham. 'Which was handy because I died on my—'

'It's not actually in the leisure centre itself,' said Miss Jolly, cutting in sharply. 'It's in the car park.'

'Oh great, so we're not even in the leisure centre, we're playing a car park,' moaned Ahmed, pressing his face up against the cold wet window.

'You lot, stay here,' said Miss Jolly as they pulled up outside the fairly rundown-looking grey concrete building. A big yellow sign shouted: 'Lose Yourself at Splashes Leisure Centre!'

'I can see how it would be very easy to lose whole years here,' joked Matt dryly. 'It's like everyone's been wiped out by a mystery virus or something.'

'Yeah, or like it's been overrun by zombies.' said Rob, rolling his eyes into the back of his head, sticking out his tongue and putting his arms out in front of his face in his best zombie pose.

'Lose yourself at the zombie leisure centre,' said Matt, putting on a weird strangulated voice

and joining in with the zombie impressions. Then Ahmed started playing the opening riff to Michael Jackson's hit 'Thriller' on his phone and the two boys stood up in the minibus and started running their 'Thriller' moves. All the other kids were laughing.

'Show them how it's done, Neil,' said Mr Gillingham, and sure enough the body-popper stood up and threw some authentic-looking shapes.

'This is the right place,' said Miss Jolly, leaning in through the front window with one hand on the hood of her anorak to prevent it from blowing off. 'But it's round the back.'

She got back in the bus and they drove round to the rear of the building. There in the car park were three large metal containers – the type you see on the back of lorries or being lifted by cranes from ships.

'We're the one in the middle. Right, everyone off,' said Miss Jolly, trying to appear positive.

'Oh jeez, I've seen everything now,' moaned Ahmed. 'We've come five hundred miles to perform in a metal box!'

'That's not helping, Ahmed,' said Mr Gillingham gruffly, and he gave the boy a gentle shove towards the 'venue'.

24

Private Dancer

Actually, like Dr Who's Tardis, the metal container seemed a lot bigger on the inside than it did on the outside, and more importantly it was dry and warm. There were ten rows of eight seats each, and at one end were some wooden pallets topped with black-painted chipboard creating a rudimentary stage. There was a pole running across the front of the stage with two black drapes at either end forming simple wings, and at the back were a couple of metal stands with three or four lights hanging off them.

'They're a load of rubbish for a start,' said Ahmed, inspecting the lights.

'Could you try to be a little more positive please, Ahmed,' said Mr Gillingham.

'Jus' sayin' good job we brought our own, sir,' he said, rather pleased with himself. 'The PA ain't bad but I've got a few bits with me that will help boost it.'

'What's that thing outside my venue?' said a voice at the door of the container. They all turned to see a wiry middle-aged man with a handlebar moustache and his hair in a topknot. He was wearing a black roll-neck jumper which matched seamlessly into black tights.

Rob nudged Matt and giggled.

'Ah,' said Mr Gillingham, going over to the door. Matt and the others followed him. The 'thing' that the odd-looking man was referring too was Ted Castle's advert for his agency. It was basically an eight-foot-wide inflatable house with a photograph of Ted himself standing in front of it and the slogan 'Every man's home should be a Castle'.

'Bit sexist,' whispered Alex.

'True,' said Miss Jolly, joining them.

'It's to do with the sponsorship of our show, I'm afraid, Mr . . .'

'Geraint Brydon,' said the man, shaking Mr Gillingham's hand limply.

'Oh, sorry,' said Miss Jolly, stepping forward to shake his hand. 'Stephanie Jolly. Forgive me, it's our first day. We're the Anglebrook School Players, up from Kent. I just wanted to have a sneaky look at the venue.'

'A school drama club, eh? Great! Takes me back! I used to love treading the boards at school. I got great notices for my Willy in *Death of a Salesman*.'

Matt and Rob burst out laughing.

Mr Gillingham gave them a sharp dig with his elbow and hissed, 'Willy is the name of the lead character in the play, you der-brains!'

Nothing could stop Geraint Brydon when he was in full flow though. 'That was before I discovered experimental dance,' he said with an exaggerated wave of his hand. 'And I never looked back. This is my twenty-third year at the Fringe. Each time I interpret a different issue of the day through the medium of dance. Last year it was cyberbullying and this year it's how we deal with a rapidly ageing population. It's called *Dement-ya*. Get it? It's a play on the word dementia,' he chuckled. 'Yes, I was quite pleased with that.'

'How's the venue?' said Mr G, following Geraint into the container.

'Oh, the venue's fine,' said Geraint. 'I mean, it's

not the Palladium. The canteen's not bad – the chips are to die for, but give the pies a wide berth. No, the main problem is the audiences.'

'Oh?' said Miss Jolly. 'What about the audiences?'

'Well, how shall I put it? They're a bit thin on the ground. We are a little off the beaten track here.'

'You can say that again,' came Ahmed's voice from behind the PA.

'How many are you getting in?' said Mr Gillingham, eager for information.

'Er ... well, my parents came last night, so that was nice. They're in their eighties now so my show's incredibly relevant to them. I gave them a lift home after – well, it's my home too in fact, so that worked out well.'

'Just your parents, or were there any others?' said Miss Jolly, exchanging a look with Mr Gillingham.

'No, just the two of them,' said Mr Brydon, nodding.

'Uh-oh, we're doomed,' chanted Ahmed.

'Ahmed, please!' snapped Mr G.

'Anyway. Look at me standing here chatting,'

said the dancer. 'You must forgive me. Mum says I could talk the hind legs off two donkeys given half a chance, and I really must be getting on – curtain up in twenty minutes. You're welcome to stay and watch?' He raised his eyebrows expectantly.

'Um ...' said Mr Gillingham, looking at Miss Jolly. 'Is it ... you know?'

'Is it what?' said Geraint.

'You know, *suitable*?' said Mr G.

'Well, it's challenging certainly, but there's no filth in it if that's what you're suggesting.'

'Perhaps another time. Lovely to meet you. We'll get out of your hair now,' interjected Miss Jolly, putting an arm round Mr Gillingham and shepherding him towards the door. She turned to the rest of the kids and clapped her hands to get their attention. 'Right, guys. Let's leave Mr Brydon to his show and go and get a cup of tea. Have a great show,' she said, turning back to him.

25
Stumbling In

They got some drinks and sat around the leisure centre cafe. Most of the gang set about running their *Othello* lines but since Matt knew the few words that the clown contributed to the play backwards, he was able to concentrate on more important matters – his set list for his first stand-up show in Edinburgh!

<u>SET LIST</u>

RUSK

BEING A KID

PARENTS CHOOSING CLOTHES

MAN-EATING HAGGIS

SHAKESPEARE UPDATED

SELFIES

TV STUFF

KENT RAP

It was a pretty disappointing turnout for the play. Basically, there were three people in the front row – Geraint Brydon and his uncle and auntie. Miss Jolly had let them in for nothing. Geraint sat munching chocolates from a big box of Milk Tray in the front row.

It was an odd feeling performing for a small crowd. With a large audience you're not doing it to anyone in particular, just to a large amorphous mass of dimly lit faces and silhouettes, but with just three people it was almost as if they were having a conversation, a one-sided conversation where the person they were talking to wasn't allowed to talk back, and they were dressed in strange clothes and wearing make-up. In other words they all felt vaguely ridiculous. Or that's how Matt felt as he went on in his clown costume. He got a couple of limp laughs from the physical bits he'd added to the script.

While he found the whole 'acting' thing enjoyable and interesting, it was nowhere near as satisfying

as stand-up comedy. He enjoyed the dressing up and the challenge of becoming someone else, and actually once he knew the lines there was a sort of satisfaction in delivering them well, but to him it felt more like a memory feat than anything particularly creative. Plus it was the same every night.

What he loved about stand-up was the freedom it gave him. At any moment during his set he could decide to break off and talk to the audience, or if a gag came to him he could just duck out of his set list for a moment and try it out. And when the laughs came he knew that they were for him alone because he was the sole creator – he was the writer, performer and director. Stand-up for Matt was the whole package.

'Loved the show,' said Geraint, grabbing Miss Jolly as soon as she emerged from the metal container. 'That boy is brilliant!'

'Neil? Othello?' she said.

'Well, he's good, and I loved the way he took that speech and turned it into a rap,' he said. 'But no, I meant your Iago.'

'Jamie? Yes, I know, he's a revelation. He's actually quite a quiet boy the rest of the time.'

'It's the quiet ones you've got to look out for,' said Geraint with a laugh. 'I think he's got real talent. One of my best friends is the head of drama at Glasgow University, and I know he's planning to come to my show at some point. I'd love him to see Jamie – I really do think he could have a bright future in this business.'

'Great, yes, I'm sure. I mean university's a long way off!'

'Soon comes round, dear! Soon comes round! Anyway, look, I'll see you tomorrow no doubt.'

After they'd got changed and removed their make-up, dismantled the set and stowed the props, there was only about ten minutes before Matt, Jamie, Neil and Alex had to start their stand-up show. There were no dressing rooms as such but they could use the toilets in the leisure centre.

More importantly for Matt there was really nowhere quiet where he could get his head together. There was only a tiny backstage area where they were jammed in like sardines.

Matt had been pretty excited for the start of the play an hour and a half earlier but it was nothing like this. This felt like electricity, everything in sharp focus. You could describe it as nervousness. He certainly had all the symptoms of being scared – his eyes were wide open, his pupils dilated, his mouth was dry, and if at that point you'd taken his pulse you would have found that his heart rate was as fast as if he'd just run the

hundred metres. But it didn't feel scary to Matt –
just exciting.

Matt, Jamie and Alex huddled in the rudimentary
wings as Neil paced up and down getting
ready to go on.

Ahmed, operating the lights and music, slowly
increased the 'audience coming in' music and faded
the house lights.

'Have a good one,' whispered Matt to Neil, who
nodded anxiously. Matt felt his phone vibrating in
the inside pocket of his jacket. He nervously fished
it out to turn it off. It informed him that he had a
text – he clicked on it distractedly.

'Good luck tonight to you and the others (but
especially you). Break a leg – but don't have a
heart attack!'

It was from Bobby Bath. Matt smiled to himself,
texted back a thumbs up, returned the phone to
his pocket, and brought the mic up to his lips to
start the show.

But as he did so, the curtain was suddenly pulled

aside. Standing there was Kitty Hope, and she didn't look very happy.

'Kit?' said Matt surprised and annoyed. 'What are you doing here? You're spoiling the surprise! Sit back down, I'm about to bring Neil on!'

Kitty's eyes filled with tears. 'There's no point, Matt,' she said. 'There's no one here!' Pulling the curtain back further, she revealed the rows of empty seats.

'But . . .' said Matt, stumbling on to the stage. 'I don't get it. It's . . . we were supposed to be doing a gig every night – a gig every night for two weeks you said. It can't be cancelled!'

26

Walk-up

'I guess it was a bit of wishful thinking on my part, you know, thinking that people would come,' said Kitty as they sat in the leisure centre canteen sharing a bowl of French fries (Geraint was right about the chips – they were knockout).

'I hadn't realised how far from the city centre the venue is, so we're not going to get much walk-up.'

'Walk-up?' asked Matt, still reeling from the disappointment of having to cancel their first show – this was like his ill-fated Sossinghurst gig all over again.

'Yes, walk-up – people who just happen to be passing, see the poster and decide to come in. People who haven't already bought their tickets in advance,' she said. 'The advantage of playing one of the big venues is if people can't get tickets to one event, they'll often buy a ticket for whatever else is playing. Anyway, we can't let this affect the show.'

'What show?' said Ahmed dryly. 'We ain't done one yet.'

'We just need to get the word out, that's all. Ideally we would have come up the day before and stuck up some posters and handed out some leaflets. We're starting from scratch.'

'I did all the social media stuff,' said Ahmed defensively. 'Problem is, it's a while since Matt's been on the box so we're not getting much traffic to the sites. What we really need is some sort of stunt.'

'A stunt?' said Matt

'Yeah, ideally a little bit of video that is funny or weird that stands a chance of going viral.'

'What sort of thing?' asked Matt.

'We could dress as the Loch Ness monster and gatecrash the Scottish Parliament,' joked Rob.

'That ain't gonna do it,' said Ahmed, shaking his head. 'It would have to be cleverer than that.'

'It's not enough just to do a good show then?' said Matt sadly.

'Well, the show has to be good – that goes without saying – but you need a reasonable number of people to see it to get the word of mouth out,' said Kitty.

'So what's the plan?'

'Tomorrow we make sure as many people know about it as possible,' said Kitty defiantly.

'You know what one of the most annoying things about cancelling today's show is?' said Matt, sitting back in his chair. 'I still haven't seen your act, Jamie!'

Jamie laughed self-consciously and shrugged. 'At this rate you may never get to see it!'

The next day Mr Gillingham drove them into the city centre.

The idea had always been to spend at least part of the day seeing the sights – the castle, Holyrood Palace, the big hill at the city's edge known as Arthur's

Seat – but Matt Millz and friends had no time for any of that. They had one mission – to get the word out about their show and they'd gone armed with a stack of posters, a bucket of wallpaper paste and a brush, and carrier bags full of photocopied leaflets.

'There's nowhere to park so I'll drop you here,' said Mr G, pulling up the minibus outside a place called the Fringe Office, which was technically the HQ of the Fringe Festival as well as being a box office where you could buy tickets for all the hundreds of shows at the Fringe.

'Careful where you put those up,' said Mr G, leaning out of the driver's window. 'Fly posting is technically illegal.'

'I think you'd better tell that to the rest of the world, Mr G,' said Matt, looking around him. Every wall, window and door seemed to have a poster on it advertising some show or other.

They agreed that Ahmed and Neil would put up posters whilst Jamie, Rob, Matt, Kitty and Alex would hand out leaflets.

'I'll pick you up from here at twelve thirty,' said Mr G, and he drove off. As the minibus pulled away Ahmed appeared from round the back of it. 'Well, that's the first one up,' he said with a grin, pointing at the bus. Sure enough he'd managed to sellotape one of their posters to the back of it.

As they stood on the pavement and gazed around them it looked like a circus. There were people on stilts, a troupe of dancers doing a routine to music

pumped out from a small speaker, a bloke in a top hat on a unicycle, plus what seemed like hundreds of people in fancy dress, and they were all doing one thing – trying to sell tickets to their shows.

'Wanna see a genuine horror story?' said a girl dressed as Elizabeth the First waving a brightly coloured leaflet in Matt's face. 'Seven thirty tonight. Watch me chop off Anne Boleyn's head for real,' she said.

'That was Henry the Eighth, wasn't it?' said Matt, taking the leaflet and looking at the graphic images. He didn't know much about history but he knew that much.

'Yeah, well we've messed around with the fabric of time so . . .' said the girl, quickly turning away and collaring someone else. 'Wanna see a genuine horror story?' she said, accosting a man in a kilt carrying some bagpipes.

'*A triumph*, said the *Scotsman*!' bellowed a bloke with a beard, his face painted silver, dressed as a robot. 'Kill to get a ticket!'

'Huh,' thought Matt. 'That would be pretty weird if people were actually killing each other just to get a ticket for this bloke's robot show.' He reached into his pocket for his little black book.

'*Love Island the Musical*!' shouted a couple of girls in bikinis. 'Tonight, half past midnight at the Pleasance!'

'I think we should go and see that,' said Ahmed, his eyes wide and his mouth open.

'This is *mad*!' said Rob with a big smile on his face.

Alex shook her head, shouting to be heard above the din. 'This is like a show in itself!'

'This, my friend, is what we're here for,' said Matt, delving into his carrier bag and handing Rob a big wedge of leaflets. 'Let's get to work!'

They all grabbed a bundle and set about trying to sell the show. 'Come and see Britain's youngest stand-up comics tonight at Splashes Leisure Centre! Splashes Leisure Centre! The venue that everyone's talking about!' shouted Matt, looking across at Rob and Kitty who were cracking up.

The leaflets were double-sided – on one side was

the advert for the school play and on the other was a smaller version of the poster for Matt's stand-up show. Matt hadn't really wanted to share leaflets but Kitty had explained how it would save money and so reluctantly he went along with it.

After about an hour they broke off and sat on the pavement taking stock.

'Well, we've put up about a quarter of the posters,' said Jamie and Neil who had come to find them. 'Problem is, as soon as we put them up someone comes and puts their posters over the top of them.'

'Well, we've handed out quite a few leaflets,' said Rob, his voice sounding a little hoarse from all the shouting.

'You need to protect your voice, Rob – we all do,' said Kitty, looking concerned.

'Yes, my voice is starting to go. Why don't we swap?' said Matt. 'You and Neil hand out leaflets. Me and Rob'll go and put up some posters?'

'Yeah, OK,' said Jamie, taking the bag of leaflets from Matt and handing Ahmed a handful.

'Come on then, Rob,' said Matt, grabbing the bucket of paste. 'Let's post some flies! I mean fly post.' Suddenly he had an image in his mind of a fly with a stamp on it being posted into a letter box, and once again reached for his little black book.

27

Cometh the Hour

By the time they got back to the leisure centre they were thoroughly worn out. They'd spent most of the day handing out leaflets, and much of it in the rain. Matt's shoes were soaked through and squelched when he walked.

They'd had about twenty minutes to relax at the hostel before being ferried to the venue. Matt was looking forward to the show though and was hopeful that the day's endeavours had paid off with a boost to audience numbers, but first he had to get through his bit of Shakespeare.

Geraint Brydon was hanging around the venue

when they got there and cornered Jamie, telling him how great he thought he'd been the day before and how he thought he would be 'going places' given the right guidance. He'd also brought his friend from Glasgow University to see the show – so at least they knew there would be two people in for *Othello* – even if one of them had seen it before.

'What do we do?' said Matt to Kitty, an hour later, after the excitement of the play was over. He had peeked round the curtain to see just eight people in the audience for the stand-up show. 'Most of them look like they're older than my grandad!'

'That's a bit ageist,' said Kitty. 'Remember Bobby Bath is in his eighties . . .'

'True,' said Matt, suitably chastised.

'I guess you've got to feel your way, Matt. I mean, you can't play it like it's the Apollo, that's for sure, but sometimes the small gigs are the best. Just think of it as every member of the audience getting a bigger slice of the show each!'

'Hmm, that's pretty smart – can I use that?' he said, reaching for his little black book.

'How's it look?' said Neil, stepping forward to join them. Over the eighteen months that had passed since Matt had first met him he'd grown taller, lost some of his 'puppy fat' and now looked a lot older than his twelve years. He was dressed in a sleek black tracksuit and white trainers.

'Eight in,' whispered Matt. 'But that's better than nothing.' At that moment Ahmed's head appeared at the front of the stage and gave them the thumbs up. 'We have clearance,' he said, checking the radio microphone was on, then handing it to Matt.

'Right,' said Matt, taking a deep breath.

'Good luck, Matt, and have a great show,' said Kitty. 'I'll be hovering at the back if you need me.'

Matt turned to see Neil, Alex and Jamie taking their places against the fire exit in the wings. They all looked extremely anxious.

Once again the lights dimmed, the music got louder, then faded to silence and Matt raised the

microphone to his lips. He felt a buzz of excitement –
it was actually happening!

'Thank you for that round of applause,' said Matt,
at which point there was a muffled laugh and the
audience started to clap. 'At last,' he said with a
laugh in his voice. He'd decided to take a leaf out
of Eddie Odillo's book and try to get a few laughs
before anyone had even been on – to help warm
the crowd up.

'Let me hear you make some noise,' he bellowed
down the mic, doing his best impression of an
American gameshow announcer. The audience
responded with claps and cheers, understanding the
gag immediately.

'Not that sort of noise,' said Matt, continuing the
impression. 'Let me hear you make the noise of an
elephant trapped in a lift.' The audience laughed
as they all tried to make the noise of what they
thought an elephant trapped in a lift might sound
like. 'Let me hear you make the noise of a giraffe
putting on a roll-neck jumper,' cried Matt. Again

GIRAFFE IN A ROLL-NECK! the audience made a whole load of disparate noises interspersed with laughter.

'And let me hear you make the sound of eight people who are out in the middle of nowhere sitting in a metal container thinking what the heck are we doing?!'

He paused – sure enough there was a big laugh as the audience suddenly became aware of the absurdity of their situation.

'But now, ladies and gentlemen, please welcome your first act. He sings, he dances, is there nothing this boy can't do? Well, yes there is – he can't cook for toffee! It's Neil Trottmaaaaaan!'

There was an enthusiastic round of applause as, bang on cue, Ahmed brought up Neil's intro track. Matt handed Neil the mic and Neil loped on.

'Whazzup, Edinboro'?' he shouted and then launched into his first routine – the rap he'd done earlier in the year at the Cavendish Hotel in the local village of Frittledean.

'He's doing well, isn't he, Matt?' It was Alex. She looked pale and was visibly shaking.

'Yeah, he gets better every time I see him. You OK?' he hissed.

'Yeah, just really nervous, that's all,' she said, blinking a tear from her big blue eyes.

'We all are,' said Matt, putting a reassuring hand on her shoulder. 'Just think of the audience as a bunch of people you'll never see again. That's what Bobby once said to me.'

'It's not just a bunch of strangers though, is it?' she said, biting her fingernails. 'It's Kit and Neil and Jamie and . . . you.'

'We're on your side, the audience will be too – just remember not to speed up,' he said, casting his mind back to the Frittledean gig, the first time they'd all shared a bill. Alex's act had been going OK until her nerves got the better of her and she'd started to race through her material – which threw her comic timing and lost the crowd completely. That was the same gig that Matt had been heckled with the line, 'Heard it!'

He'd learned his lesson that night and his new set was literally all pretty much untried and untested. It was a big risk to go out not knowing how any of the gags were going to fly, but Matt knew that the whole purpose of the trip was for him to try out some stuff and end up with a good tight fifteen to twenty minutes of material that no one had seen him do before.

Matt shuddered as he thought back to the review of that show the following day in the local paper – it had virtually written him off as a lame duck, a flash in the pan. In many ways this show was the start of his comeback – and boy was he determined to make it work.

Neil, meanwhile, was getting good rounds of applause at the end of each routine.

'Here we go,' whispered Matt as he recognised the start of Neil's final rap, which was a semi-serious piece all about his music heroes. 'Not long now!'

Alex gulped and looked at the back of her hand where she'd written her set list – a trick she'd picked up from Matt, who in turn had seen Eddie Odillo do it.

Onstage, Neil was finishing up:

'. . . Grandmaster Flash, Dr Dre –
ain't many rappers made me feel this way,
From Afrika Bambaataa to Jay Z
I'm happy when I'm rapping,
The only way I can be me . . .'

As he finished he thrust the mic into the air – unfortunately he'd only ever practised this move at home, which it turned out had a slightly higher ceiling than the venue he was in now. The mic rebounded off the metal ceiling with a clang. And hit Neil on the head!

'Ow!' he cried and sank to his knees – to a massive laugh and a round of applause.

'You should keep that in,' whispered Matt as Neil handed him the mic in the wings.

Neil rolled his eyes and clutched his head. 'Think I'm gonna get a bump,' he said.

Matt made a split-second decision to capitalise on the audience's good mood and get Alex straight on. He nodded to her, then started the announcement. 'Neil Trottman there, ladies and gents – proving there's no ceiling to his talents, apart from the one he bounces the mic off!'

He grinned at Jamie, who smiled back. He was pleased with that ad-lib.

'But now please welcome a woman of a thousand voices – it's Alex Williams!'

He handed the mic to Alex, who held up both hands to show crossed fingers. She smiled weakly, tossed back her hair and strode on to the stage to a good round of applause.

'Hello there,' she said with a big 'please-like-me' smile. 'It's great to be in Scotland – or should I say, in the words of Nicola Spurgeon. 'Och awae, tis arn a hoo the noo!' Nicola Spurgeon was the head of the Scottish parliament, so it got a good laugh of recognition. Then Alex's gig took a slight turn for the worse.

'Steady there, ya wee sassenach,' came a lone voice with a thick Scottish accent from up the back.

'Uh-oh!' thought Matt, exchanging a worried look with Jamie standing next to him. 'We've got a heckler in.' Matt had talked Alex through a couple of fairly standard heckle put-down lines – he just hoped she wouldn't panic.

It was now his turn to cross his fingers. If she didn't deal with him straight away he could turn the whole show.

Alex paused for a moment and turned to look at Matt in the wings. Matt made a punching motion with his fist and mouthed 'Get him!', willing her to see the heckler off. Alex turned back to the crowd and cleared her throat.

'No offence,' she said, putting her hands on her hips, 'but is that your real face or are you getting ready for Halloween?'

There was a huge laugh, which she took as her cue to get back to her act. Actually the heckler had done her a favour. It meant that the audience now trusted her, and more importantly liked her, and the rest of her impressions – although patchy, with one or two slow bits – went over much better than her debut at the Cavendish.

'Is that your set list?' said Matt, leaning to take a look over Jamie's shoulder at the papers he was studying.

Jamie nodded, quickly folded them back into his inside pocket, then stepped away from Matt, but not before Matt had caught sight of a few bits. It was all typed out on printed sheets.

'Looks more like a script than a set list,' said Matt, surprised. He wasn't being nosy; he was genuinely interested in how Jamie worked.

'Yeah, I guess it is a kind of script. I like to type the whole thing out, word for word, then learn it like I would a monologue. Same process as with the play,' he said, looking past Matt at Alex onstage. She was just going into the last couple of minutes of her Theresa March routine, so Matt and Jamie knew it would shortly be Jamie's turn.

'Doesn't that limit you a bit?' asked Matt. 'I mean, if it's one long monologue, don't you find that if you break out of it or think of something else you want to say, you lose your place?'

'I don't,' said Jamie.

'Don't what?' said Matt. 'Don't lose your place?'

He could tell he was beginning to wind the other boy up so stepped away from him, knowing how important it was to concentrate on your act before going on. Comedians call it getting 'in the zone'.

He was a little perplexed though. He'd never heard of any other comedian working like that. Most comics had a list of routines and gags and a rough order in which they planned to tell them, knowing that the order could change on any given night. The actual wording of the routines was flexible too – maybe to incorporate someone in the audience or something that happened on the night. Although Matt had only limited experience, he knew that one of the keys to being a good comic was being able to think on your feet.

There was a good smattering of applause as Alex finished up and at least she was smiling this time as she headed towards Matt in the wings. The last time she'd been in tears.

'Well done,' said Matt, taking the mic off her.

'Thank God that's over. I need some fresh air,' she said, her face bright red and her hair sticking to her forehead with sweat. Then she turned to Jamie and whispered, 'It's really hot out there.' And she pushed open the emergency exit into the cool Edinburgh afternoon.

Matt knew that he had to act quickly, to get Jamie on before the applause died down, to maintain whatever momentum the show had built up.

'Alex Williams, ladies and gentlemen!' bellowed Matt, turning to Jamie and nodding. Jamie nodded nervously back.

'Right, ladies and gents, you're in for a treat. Making his Edinburgh debut – just like all the other acts tonight – please welcome, from Kent, Jamie Castle!'

He handed the mic to Jamie who strode towards the centre of the makeshift stage.

Suddenly a change came over him. He went from being the slightly shy, quiet boy that they all knew, to a confident, almost brash comic. He now looked and sounded like he'd been doing stand-up comedy all his life!

'Hey! Thanks for waiting!' he said cheekily. 'Great to be here! Hey, who's got a cat here?' He looked down at the few faces in the audience. No one put their hand up or volunteered any information so he pointed to someone in the front row. 'You, madam, do you have a cat?'

The woman shrunk back in her seat, her body language screaming that she didn't want to get involved, and shook her head.

'No?' asked Jamie. 'But tell me, do you like cats?'

The woman nodded. 'Yes,' she said.

'So get a cat,' said Jamie. 'Is that so hard?'

There was a massive laugh.

'So what else do you like that you haven't got?'

said Jamie.

There was another massive laugh.

'So I have a dog ...' he continued, moving to the other side of the stage, much to the relief of the woman who liked cats but didn't have one. 'I have a dog, and whenever there's someone at the door, my dog runs at the door, barking.' He bent over, not quite on all fours, but basically acting like he was the dog, running at the front door. 'Ruff! Ruff! Ruff!' he said, barking like a dog.

There was another massive laugh.

'Woof! Woof! Woof! Woof!' he said, changing the barking noise slightly, which inexplicably made it funnier.

Another laugh.

'Rar! Rar! Rar! Rar!' he went, changing the noise again, and all the while the laughs were building. He then straightened up to his full height.

'But you know what?' he said, pausing for comic effect. 'Whoever's at the door, it's never for my dog! It's never for him!'

This time the laugh was even bigger and was accompanied by a smattering of applause.

Matt, watching from the wings, felt a dull ache in his throat that he knew was jealousy.

'He's great isn't he?' said Kitty, joining him from the emergency exit and nudging up against him. 'I just don't know where it comes from!'

'Indeed,' thought Matt. 'Where *did* it all come from?' Jamie Castle – a twelve-year-old boy who had never done a proper gig before – was strutting around the stage like an old pro, each gag building on the last. There was no hint of a lull or a punchline going wrong or failing to get a laugh. No, Jamie was delivering carefully crafted routines that would have taken Matt months to put together.

The dog routine gave way to a great routine about the self-checkout machines in supermarkets.

'You know, sometimes what I like to do is load up a big trolley full of food and wine and just start checking it out – *bip*!' He acted the noise that the checkout makes as it reads the barcode. 'Bip!' He carried on in this vein. Matt knew it as the comedy of repetition, the idea that, to a point, the more you repeated something the funnier it got – provided you had a killer punchline to finish it off.

'Bip!' went Jamie. Then again. 'Bip! Yeah, I check out a whole trolley, then I go and load up another trolley full and do the same. Bip! … Bip! … just to see how long it is before someone from the store comes and tries to stop me!' Another huge gale of laughter ensued.

At that point it dawned on Matt what the other thing was that was so weird about Jamie's material. While Matt's was all based on stuff he'd seen and heard – stuff about his parents, about school life and so on – Jamie's stuff, rather than being the musings of a thirteen-year-old boy, was all from the adult world.

'I've been Jamie Castle! Thanks for watching!' he said with a wave of his hand, then he turned and stepped the few feet it took to get off the stage and into the wings.

From the moment he'd picked up the microphone to his closing gag some fifteen minutes later, it had been wall-to-wall laughs. The audience had loved him and now they had their chance to show just how much.

There was only one word for it. An eruption. The audience erupted into as much noise as eight people can make with just their hands, their feet and their voices, and it completely knocked Matt for six, leaving him reeling.

As Jamie had walked on, Matt had been curious in a detached way, but had felt confident that there was no way, just *no way* that with a complete lack of stand-up experience Jamie could be anything other than average at best. He hadn't expected, in his wildest dreams, that Jamie would be so good. It had been dynamite! Matt had assumed too much and suddenly here he was having to go on after him.

'Wow! That was ...' Matt stuttered as Jamie handed him the mic.

Jamie shrugged – suddenly he was back to being the quiet, shy boy of just fifteen minutes ago.

Kitty stepped straight in and gave Jamie a hug. 'That was just great, Jamie,' she said, flinging her arms round him in an uncharacteristically demonstrative display of emotion.

'Jeez,' muttered Ahmed to Matt as he joined him in the wings. 'Follow that!'

Matt didn't need to be told. The usual nerves he'd been feeling about going on were suddenly multiplied tenfold. The focus he'd had up until Jamie had gone on had now just flown out of the window. Put simply, his mind was a jumble. In a flash he remembered Eddie Odillo's support act at the Palladium and how Kitty had told him the star act made sure no one before them was too good.

'Er . . . mate,' said Ahmed giving Matt a sharp dig in the ribs.

'Yeah?' said Matt, trying to pull himself together and concentrate on his act.

'You need to get out there, mate. It's your turn,' said his friend, indicating the stage with his thumb.

Ahmed was right. The applause for Jamie's act had finished and the audience were now staring silently at an empty stage. Matt brought the mic up to his lips and spoke.

'Er . . . Jamie . . . Jamie Castle there! But now please welcome your final act tonight – me! I mean, Matt Millz!'

Thankfully there was a really good response to his name, a strong round of applause and even one or two cheers as Matt walked out to meet his audience. He glanced back and could see Jamie silhouetted in the light coming through the emergency exit, chatting animatedly to Alex, Kitty and Ahmed.

28

Sixty-Four-Thousand-Dollar Man

'If you've enjoyed tonight,' said Matt, finishing up, 'please tell your friends. If you didn't, keep it to yourself! I'm Matt Millz, that's all from me, goodnight!' he said, signing off in his usual way to a good solid round of applause, but Matt was acutely aware that it was nothing like the response they'd given Jamie.

His act had gone pretty well, and most importantly he'd tried out a whole load of new stuff, much of which got good laughs. If he had to put a hit rate on it he'd say it was maybe sixty–forty good to not so good, with maybe ten per cent just plain not funny.

Even with the bad stuff he could see what he needed to do to make it work.

But if he was honest, it never truly lifted off and got beyond a 'work in progress' gig, and following Jamie's barnstormer of a set hadn't helped. All the time he'd been onstage he could hear a nagging voice in the back of his mind saying, 'How did Jamie get so good?'

'Great job,' said Kitty as he passed her in the wings, but he ignored her and carried on through the emergency exit and into the car park.

He kept on walking until he got to the perimeter, where he sat down on the low metal barrier and took a deep breath. He was annoyed at himself for letting the way Jamie's act had gone down rattle him. A comedy bill shouldn't be a competition – but that's exactly how it had felt to Matt. He'd taken his position as top comic for granted, pure and simple.

Just where had it all come from though? Was there such a thing as a comedy genius, and if so was that what Jamie Castle was? For Matt, that was the sixty-four-thousand-dollar question.

'Are you going to come and help tidy up then?' said Mr Gillingham, wandering over to find him.

'Yes, sir, sorry, sir,' said Matt, looking up at his teacher. 'I was pulling myself together. I haven't done a gig for so long, I was a little rusty . . .'

'It was great, Matt – really good to see you back doing what you do so well,' said Mr G, giving him an encouraging pat on the shoulder as they walked back to the container. 'You took a lot of risks when you could have played it safe, I really admire you for that,' he said. 'You've got a brilliant comic mind and I can't wait to see where you get to by the end of two weeks – it's very exciting. I know how much this means to you.'

'Thanks, sir,' shrugged Matt, cheering up a bit. 'If I'm honest, Jamie's act threw me rather.'

'I think it surprised all of us,' said Mr G with a laugh in his voice. 'It won't do you any harm to have a little competition though,' he said wryly. 'And I hope you congratulated him on how well it went.'

Mr G was right – praise where it was due.

'No, I haven't seen him properly to talk to.'

'Well, be sure you do that. The audience got a really good show tonight and that's down to all four of you, not one single act. You should all be proud of yourselves.'

'Cheers, sir. I'll do that now,' said Matt, breaking into a run and heading to join the others at the metal container.

'I thought you were fab tonight, Jamie,' said Magda as they tucked into what they had decided would become their regular post-show feast of French fries in the Splashes canteen. 'Totally owned it! Gave Matt a run for his money, eh, Matt? Ouch!' Rob had clearly kicked her under the table.

'It's fine,' said Matt a little wearily. 'Magda's right, you were easily the funniest on the bill, Jamie, right?' The others nodded and made noises in agreement.

'Gotta hand it to you, Jamie. It was all killer and no filler,' said Ahmed, exchanging a fist pump with him.

'Oh, thanks, Ahmed. I really enjoyed myself,' said Jamie, smiling but oddly avoiding eye contact.

'Which is great news for the show,' said Matt. 'But you know what?' he added playfully. 'Watch out, Jamie! I'm coming after you! I'm really looking forward to tomorrow night!'

'I thought you were great tonight too, Matt,' said Jamie to Matt. 'I don't know where you come up with ideas.'

'Same place as you, I guess,' said Matt.

'What do you mean?' said Jamie. Did Matt detect a hint of defensiveness in his voice?

'Well, you know, from everyday life, stuff I see on TV, hear on the radio or see on Instagram,' Matt explained.

'Yes, yes of course. Yeah everything's a possible source for gags,' agreed Jamie. 'And let's not forget the play. I thought the play was good tonight too.'

'I'd like to forget the play ...' said Rob, rolling his eyes.

'You were great, Neil,' said Jamie.

'Raise your glasses to the rapping Othello!' said Matt, clinking glasses with the others. Neil nodded and took the opportunity to cram a fistful of chips into his mouth.

'You too, Alex,' said Jamie.

'You're right, it was fun tonight,' said Alex. 'Actually it was the first time I kind of got what the whole story was about!'

29
Read All About It

They spent the next morning handing out leaflets and fly posting, then had their packed lunch on a bench in the festival gardens before returning to the venue for the play and the quick turnaround to the comedy show.

Matt was excited at the prospect of another gig so hot on the heels of the last – it meant he could act on all the ideas and tweaks he'd come up with from the night before, plus, if it went well, he was planning to throw in a few new bits.

This time there were twelve people waiting when Kitty opened the doors. 'Word's getting out!' she said excitedly as she joined Matt in the wings. 'Twelve in. It's building!'

'I hope you're right, Kit,' said Matt, only daring to hope that one day the venue might be full.

All the acts went down slightly better than the night before, which meant that once again Jamie's act raised the roof – making it even harder for Matt to establish himself afterwards.

And so it went on. Each day the audiences grew and Matt built on the experiences of the day before, as did the others – Neil and Alex. All of them, except Jamie. Jamie's act stayed word for word exactly the same. Every line, every move – for Matt it was like watching a video of the night before.

Post-show, Matt would run through his set list, looking at what had gone well, what hadn't, what should be chucked out and what needed work and how he could fix it – he loved that part of the show almost as much as doing his act.

'Why don't you try out some new bits?' said Matt

to Jamie after the show one night as they were tucking into a basket of French fries.

'Huh? New bits? Why would I do that?' said Jamie. As the week had worn on he'd started to become a little cocky – more like his onstage persona.

'Well, you've nailed that fifteen minutes, so don't you want to expand it?' said Matt. 'Try out some new material?'

'Why trouble trouble?' said Jamie, shrugging off the idea. 'This works so why mess with it?'

Well, he was right about one thing. It did work. It always, one hundred per cent, killed.

They'd done six shows when Ahmed walked into the Splashes canteen waving a newspaper.

'Hey! Millz!' he said, walking towards the others at their usual table. 'We got a review!'

'For the play?' said Jamie excitedly.

'For both,' said Ahmed, sitting down and opening the paper on the table at the review section and spreading its pages wide. They all gathered round as Ahmed started to read them out. The play got three stars, with special mention for Neil and Alex and, of course, Jamie – the reviewer was particularly impressed with Jamie. It seemed the same writer had hung around for the stand-up show too.

'OK, here we go. Ready?' said Ahmed, flexing the newspaper between his hands, enjoying the power he had over the others.

'Just get on with it,' said Rob, trying to grab the paper from him.

'How many stars?' said Jamie excitedly.

'Four!' said Ahmed.

'Yes!' exclaimed Neil, punching the air excitedly.

'Come on then, Ahmed – what's it say?' said Matt.

'"*Matt Millz and Friends*, Splashes Leisure Centre, Leith.

'"This reviewer didn't know quite what to expect as he sat waiting in the metal container that houses this comedy bill featuring some of the kids who had appeared in *Othello* just half an hour before, but if I was their teacher I'd be giving them full marks! The show's host may be familiar to fans of *The T Factor* – where he got his first bite of fame and is indeed billed as 'The youngest comic to ever raise the roof at the Hammersmith Apollo'. That may be true but he's got some stiff competition on this bill if tonight was anything to go by.

'"Matt generated a very genial atmosphere from the start—"'

'*Genial?*' said Matt. 'I was hoping for a bit more than *genial*!'

Ahmed read on:

'"... working the crowd nicely and laying the groundwork for the first act, Neil Trottman. Trottman is a rapper who at the tender age of just eleven shows huge promise. He moves well and "spits" his lyrics with total concentration – clearly believing every word. Covering topics such as the ignominy of having to be in bed by nine o'clock—"'

'Igno— what?' said Magda, shaking her head.

'—nominy!' said Kitty. 'We're all doing it for no money. It's not just Neil,' she tutted.

"'. . . to an actually quite moving litany of the musicians that have inspired him, Trottman was the perfect start to the show.'"

'Happy with that!' said Neil, nodding his head and fishing his phone out to text his mum the good news.

"'Talented mimic Alex Williams was next and she delivered a fairly narrow selection of famous voices with uncanny precision. Some of the material was a little so-so but this can only improve with experience. All in all a confident Edinburgh debut.'"

'Phew!' said Alex, sitting back in her chair. 'Sounds like I got away with it!'

'You more than got away with it, Alex,' said Kitty. 'There's some good quotes there, for the future.'

"'Away from his hosting duties, Matt Millz offered us a robust fifteen-minute set—"'

'Hang on!' interjected Matt. 'How come they've missed out Jamie?'

'Don't worry, that's coming!' said Ahmed. '"... demonstrating a quick mind, enviable imagination and great comic timing."'

'Result!' said Rob, high-fiving Matt.

'"Millz shows real promise, although he lacked a bit of polish and some of the routines could certainly do with an edit."'

'Fair enough!' said Matt. 'That's what I'm here for after all!'

Ahmed looked up from the paper. 'Ready, Jamie?'

Jamie nodded and Ahmed read on.

'"The surprise star of the show however" ...' said Ahmed, pausing for effect, '"was Jamie Castle—"'

'Wit woo!' said Magda, giving Jamie a playful shove.

'"... whose timeless routines made happy laughter absolutely effortless. Although not demonstrating Millz's daring and flights of fancy, he generated big broad laughs on mature topics such as the correct way to stack a dishwasher and household pets. This kid is surely a big star for the future. Although Master Millz tops the bill, there's no doubt who the real headliner is – Jamie Castle.'"

There was a stunned silence as Ahmed finished reading and placed the newspaper on the table.

'Coulda been worse. You should see the review for the old bloke in before us,' said Ahmed. 'He only gets one star!'

'Poor Mr Brydon,' said Alex with a frown.

'Nice one, Jamie,' said Matt magnanimously, but there was no hiding his disappointment.

'Everyone got a really good review,' said Kitty, standing. 'And to celebrate, I'm going to order another bowl of chips!' There was a roar of approval from everyone round the table. All, that is, except Matt.

'Not for me, Kitty. I think I'll go and get some fresh air …' he said, and with that he stood up and walked out of the canteen.

'Ouch!' said Rob under his breath.

30
Dog Eat Dog

The next day, Matt and Rob decided to try and put some posters up a little further away from the Fringe Office, as virtually every square inch seemed to be already covered in flyers, often several layers thick.

'This looks like a good spot!' cried Matt, darting down a cobblestoned back alley with Rob following behind him. When they got there, someone had beaten them to it.

'*The Comedy Bunker*' screamed the poster in black letters flecked with green neon. 'Featuring Dave Khan, Stacy Long, Brendan O'Sullivan and Dolisa Adefope.'

'Looks like a good show actually,' said Matt; he'd seen a couple of them on *Stand-up at the Apollo*. 'Shame to have to cover it up, but it's dog eat dog here, I'm afraid!' He slapped a brush full of wallpaper paste across it. Rob then unrolled one of their *Matt Millz and Friends* posters and slid it up over the competition.

'Hang on a sec,' said Rob, stepping back to look at it. 'It's not straight!' He then set about adjusting it, gliding it on the thick slimy paste.

'We haven't got time for that,' laughed Matt. 'It's not an art exhibition. We've still got to get all this lot up.'

'You've got to have pride in your work,' said Rob, fishing out his iPhone. 'Just stand next to it and let's get a photo!'

Matt stood next to the poster and pulled a face as Rob fiddled with his phone. 'Agh! It's stuck in video mode, hang on!' Just then there was a screech of tyres, the slam of a car door and a gruff voice called out from behind them.

'Oi! You two!' It was followed by the click of Cuban heels on cobblestones. It was a voice that Matt immediately recognised. He spun round to see a figure in a long leather coat, leather trousers and cowboy boots. The man's pock-marked skin was pale like that of someone who preferred life in the shadows and was surmounted by a greying quiff, making him look to all the world like a sort of rockabilly vampire. It was, of course, none other than the slimy agent with whom Matt had history, Dickie Hart.

'You!' said the man through curled lips and narrowing his eyes. 'I thought I'd seen the last of you!'

Matt shuddered and swallowed hard. 'Hello, Mr Hart,' he said meekly. His heart was pounding – there was something about this man's coldness that was truly sinister.

'You've stuck your poster over one of mine, you idiots,' snarled Dickie. 'Take it down now!'

Matt looked at Rob and hesitated, not knowing quite what to do.

'Er ... fair enough, I s'pose,' he said and reached up to peel the poster off.

'No, Matt!' said Rob, looking Dickie Hart squarely in the eye.

'Didn't you 'ear me?' said Dickie, narrowing his eyes to a squint. 'Take it down! NOW!'

'Or what?' said Rob.

'Or I'll take it down for you,' growled Dickie, taking a step forward towards the boys.

'Then I'll call the police,' came another familiar voice from behind them as Mr Gillingham appeared from a side alley. He was a big man, an ex-rugby player, and Dickie Hart knew when he'd met his match.

'Huh!' he said. 'What would the police do?'

'Quite possibly charge you with fly posting, which due to subsection four, paragraph two of the Highways Act is illegal and punishable with a hefty fine,' glared Mr G.

'But they're doin' it too,' said Dickie, pointing at the boys, a little confused.

'They're kids, minors – they'd probably get away with a bit of a telling-off, but you . . . ? You're old enough to know better, and it's not your first offence either, is it? You've got posters all over town!' said Mr G. There was a beat while Dickie's brain took in the information and balanced up his options.

'Yeah, well, I don't suppose anyone'll come to see a show with a bunch of kids in it, anyway. You can do with all the help you can get! Her-her!' he sniggered. 'But I'm warning you. If I catch you at it again I won't be responsible for my actions!' Then he turned on his very expensive heel and with a swish of his leather coat wandered back to his waiting limo.

'Who was that?' said Mr G, joining the boys.

'His name is Dickie Hart, sir,' said Matt. 'A nasty piece of work – he's the agent that took me on for a few days last year when I was a having a bit of a crisis. Took me on and took me to the cleaners too.'

'Classic bully,' said Mr G, watching as the car trundled across the cobblestones. 'Full of aggression when he's faced with a smaller prey but collapses like a house of cards when faced with someone his own size. Anyway, I came to tell you that you've got half an hour, then we need to be getting back, so if you're going to do any more illegal fly posting you'd better get on with it!'

'I was very impressed with your knowledge of the Highways Act, sir,' said Matt with a grin.

'Oh, I made all that up,' laughed Mr G. 'I mean, do I look like the sort of bloke who's learned the Highways Act?'

'Matt?' said Kitty as the boys joined the rest of the

group outside the Fringe Office.

'Yeah?' said Matt. He could tell from her face that something was wrong.

'Have you been up to something?' she said, looking at her phone. It kept pinging repeatedly. 'It's just that I've had seventy-five texts in the last five minutes from journalists asking for a comment.'

'Hey, Rob!' It was Ahmed, and he too was clutching his phone. 'Nice one!'

'I'm sorry, Ahmed, what do you mean, nice one?'

'Your video, of that prat warning you off sticking posters up – it's gone viral! It's gonna make us a hit!'

It turned out that after Rob had posted the video of Dickie Hart threatening them, it had been picked up by some of the Fringe Festival community, who were now holding up the incident as an example of how the festival had changed from its founding principles of individuals putting on shows for all the best reasons – for art, for fun and not necessarily to make money and a career. It also turned out there was a lot of bad feeling towards big promoters like Dickie Hart's agency Excalibur, who had squeezed out the smaller performers – the one-man bands, the amateurs and semi-pros like Geraint Brydon – from the big venues and hiked up the prices. Two kids promoting their own production of *Othello* and a stand-up show being threatened by the head of one of those big promoters seemed, for many, to sum up the whole issue in a nutshell.

'That, my friend is what I meant by a stunt,' said Ahmed with a big grin.

'This is dynamite!' said Kitty.

'She's right,' said Ahmed, nodding. 'You couldn't pay for press like this. Gotta hand it to you, bruv – you did my job for me!'

'There's a lot of press interest,' said Kitty, excitedly peering at her phone. 'BBC Scotland want to do a quick interview at the venue before the show tonight!'

'Fantastic,' said Matt – it seemed Dickie Hart's attempt to kill off their show had completely backfired.

31

Back on the Box

'Social media sites have been buzzing today with a short video of two schoolboys who appear to be threatened with physical violence while trying to advertise their show at the Edinburgh Festival,' said the woman in a raincoat, clutching a microphone. 'For many, this sums up just what has gone wrong with the festival in recent years, as corporate business has moved in and stifled much of the creativity that the Fringe was originally built on. I'm here now at Splashes Leisure Centre with the two boys, Matthew Mills and Robert Brown.'

The shot widened to reveal Matt and Rob

grinning broadly outside their metal container. Behind them was a poster that Ahmed had hastily put up before the interview started, advertising their show.

'How are you feeling?' said the woman, poking the mic into Matt's face.

'It was pretty scary at the time,' said Matt. 'Wasn't it, Rob?'

'Yeah, because he's like a man and we're just, well, smaller . . .' His voice tailed off.

'He's still in shock,' said Matt, indicating Rob. 'I don't know what we would have done if Mr Gillingham hadn't come along – he's our teacher. You know, we might be in hospital now or worse . . .' he added, really trying to milk the situation for all it was worth.

'So you were scared for your lives?'

'Yes, terrified. I still have nightmares . . .' Then, realising his mistake, he continued, 'You know, like, waking nightmares where Mr Hart is standing over me, threatening me about our posters and

trying to kill off our show!' He turned away from
the interviewer to face the camera. 'Which is on
here at Splashes Leisure Centre every day at four
thirty, tickets ten pounds, or seven pounds fifty for
concessions!'

'How's the show been going, Matt?' said the lady.

'Well, to be honest it's been a bit slow – until today,'
he said and stuck his hand out. The camera swung
round to reveal a huge queue of people waiting to get
in to their metal box.

'So it looks like Mr Hart's nasty behaviour hasn't
paid off,' said the interviewer with a self-satisfied
smile. 'Adele Parffit, BBC News, Edinburgh.'

As she finished up they all relaxed. 'That was great, lads,' said Ms Parffit as the camera crew started to pack up the camera and equipment. 'Bit of a cheeky plug, but never mind, you deserve to do well after that.'

'Thanks for your interest,' said Kitty, stepping in and handing her one of her business cards.

'Well, we've got to dash,' said the reporter. 'We're due across town to cover the nominations for the Wetfizz Awards.'

'What was she talking about just then, Kit?' said Matt as they wandered round the back of the metal container to get ready.

'The Wetfizz Awards? Surely you know about them?' she said. 'It's a big deal for all Edinburgh comics.'

'Wetfizz? The bottled water? You mentioned that before, something about an award? Why would comics be interested in an award for spring water?'

'Wetfizz are the sponsors. It's a comedy award – and it's a massive deal. The winner gets twenty-five thousand pounds, which obviously is pretty cool, but the big thing is the career boost a comic gets from it, from all the press and industry buzz,' she said excitedly. 'You know, the Edinburgh Festival is a massive showcase and all the TV people come up every year looking for the next big thing. They even have an actual TV festival up here next weekend so they can all be in the right place for when the result of the Wetfizzes are announced.'

'Think there's any chance . . . ?' said Matt hopefully.

'Bit of a long shot, Matt, but you never know,' she said with a stoical grin. 'I'm not sure the Wetfizz judges get out as far as Splashes Leisure Centre.'

As Matt and the others waited behind the black curtain to go on just ten minutes later, Kitty popped her head round the emergency exit brimming with excitement.

'Matt! Matt! It's sold out!' she squealed.

'What?' said Matt, taking a moment for the news to sink in.

'Eighty paying punters!'

He pulled back the curtain slightly to take a peek. Sure enough the place was packed! There were even a few people standing at the back.

'We're a hit!' said Kitty, and for once she allowed her usual calm exterior to slip, scrunching one hand into a tiny fist and punching the air. 'We're a freakin' hit!'

32
When the Chips Are Down...

Having honed their skills on tiny audiences, suddenly the young performers found that with a sell-out crowd their acts were transformed. What had previously gone down moderately well, now got huge waves of laughter and applause – and in Jamie's case cheers! In fact, as Matt walked out after Jamie, the audience were on their feet and calling for more – something that Matt found incredibly difficult to deal with. He found himself having to calm them down before launching into his own act, which was far from ideal.

Once he'd got going he'd had a whale of a time. The big laughs meant that, for the first time, he had time to think about what he was going to say next and to come up with ad-libs – which inevitably might end up staying in the act.

'My name's Matt Millz! I hope you've enjoyed tonight – if you did, please tell your friends. If you didn't, keep it to yourself! Goodnight!' he finished, not to a standing ovation, but to a big round of applause and a few cheers, and he was happy with that. By now he had got used to not going down as well as Jamie.

Laughs add time, and because of the huge audience response the timings for the whole show spread. Instead of being exactly one hour long it came in at an hour and a quarter, an issue that Kitty was quick to address at the post-show chip feast.

'I talked to the box office and we're sold out again tomorrow night,' she said with a proud smile.

'Way to go!' chirruped Ahmed.

'And the night after that. In fact, we're heading towards selling out the rest of the run!'

'Extend it!' joked Matt. 'Let's never go home!'

'The show that's in the venue after us were very good about the overrun today, but we've got to be practical – we can't do it again. So look, we need to make a few changes – everyone needs to cut five minutes off their act.'

'What!' said Matt. 'You're joking?'

'I'm not joking, we need to make trims.'

'I can't cut my act down – I've learned it as a whole,' said Jamie, looking anxious.

'Yes, I know, and since you're getting such a good response I don't think that's a good idea anyway. If they're asking for more, the last thing we should do is give them less. So Jamie, you can carry on doing what you're doing.'

Jamie nodded. Matt couldn't believe his ears. This whole venture had been pushed through to get *him* stage time and now here he was being asked to cut back his act! It was true that every night Jamie had stormed it and Matt had had difficulty following him, but Matt felt that his act was really beginning to take shape – he was on the verge of a real breakthrough.

'Can I have a quick word, Kit?' said Matt after the chips were all gone and the meeting had broken up. Kitty followed him out of the canteen and round to the play area.

'Yes, Matt? What's up?' she said climbing on to one of the swings.

'What's up?' said Matt, easing himself on to the one next to hers. '*What's up?* I don't think I should have to cut back my act, that's what's up!'

'OK, so you might not like what I'm going to say next then. I don't know how to put this . . .' she said warily. 'First of all, I don't think you should take it in any way as an insult to you or your act or what you've been achieving . . .'

'Sounds ominous,' said Matt, looking her squarely in the eyes. Something was wrong. Kitty was not one to beat around the bush – her directness, although sometimes a little difficult to take, was one of the things that Matt admired most about her. 'What shouldn't I be insulted by?' he said, peering at her over his glasses.

She sighed and took a deep breath, as if stealing herself to break some bad news. 'I think Jamie should close the show,' she said. 'Sorry, I know it's not what you – I mean, we – had in mind, but Jamie's going down so well, it's making it hard for you to follow him and it's upsetting the shape of the show. It's not that his act's any better than yours – it's just different and the way the show is working out it would be better if he followed you.' She spoke as if she'd been rehearsing her little speech for a while.

Matt shook his head and looked down at the ground as it moved back and forth under the swing then put his hand through his quiff. He was lost for words – but not for long.

'But it's called *Matt Millz and Friends*,' he said, turning to her with a look of desperation.

'Ah, well I know, I've thought about that. I was thinking maybe you should go on first . . .'

'First?!' exclaimed Matt. That really was an insult. Had her opinion of his skills sunk so low?

'Hear me out,' she snapped a little harshly. 'I'm suggesting – and we don't have to do it if you're dead against it – you go on first, do five, then bring on Neil, then bring on Alex after him . . .'

'What, you mean be the MC?' he said. They both knew that the MC's job, while important, was something of a thankless task. It didn't hold anywhere near the prestige of being one of the acts; in fact many people who went to comedy gigs came away not really thinking of the MC as an act at all. They often thought that they were just the manager of the club, or the promoter.

'Hang on,' she said, pulling him up again. 'You'd be *like* an MC, in that you'd bring on the other acts, but the critical difference is you'd *then* do your set slightly cut down, but overall you'd still be doing the full fifteen minutes. At the end you'd bring Jamie on to close the show and maybe come on at the very end to wind it up too? That way it's still Matt Millz and friends. Plus you get to do as long, and you get a chance to develop your audience skills – so that by the time you come on to do your shortened set, hopefully the audience know you and it'll go even better than it has been so far.'

Matt thought about it for a moment. As hard as it was for him to give up his headliner spot he could see that what Kitty was suggesting actually made a lot of sense. If he was completely honest with himself, it would take some of the pressure off him too. He couldn't deny that having to follow Jamie every night was really just adding another whole level of stress.

'To be honest, Kit,' he said, 'following Jamie has been really stressing me out. Let's go with your idea. I'm fine with it. You're right, the show comes first and you know what? It might be fun.'

'That's really understanding of you, Matt, thanks,' she said, putting her arm round him and giving him a squeeze.

33

A Very Pleasant Encounter

Although the rest of the shows were looking like a sell-out, the gang were still keen to go out and publicise it. Besides, they still had a whole stack of posters and leaflets. Mr Gillingham dropped them in their usual place on the hill outside the Fringe Office, and the seasoned fly-posting team of Matt and Rob walked up the steep hill looking for somewhere new to glue their posters.

'What's that place?' said Rob, pointing across a busy road at a large granite archway with huge hoardings either side bedecked with posters advertising shows. As they got closer Matt read the sign above the arch. 'The Pleasance,' he said. 'I've heard of that – it's on a lot of the posters, and it's mainly stand-ups!'

'Well, maybe we should—' But before Rob could finish his sentence Matt had run across the road and was under the arch. Through the archway was a cobbled courtyard which was teeming with people. There was a huge queue snaking towards a doorway to the left of them, another to the right and another over the other side of the courtyard leading to a huge bar. The Pleasance, it turned out, was one of the oldest venues of the Fringe and in fact housed seventeen venues all on one sprawling plot.

'Don't move a muscle,' said Matt, with eyes wide. 'I've just seen Romesh Ranganathan!' They both stared in wonder as the popular TV comic wandered past having an animated discussion with a woman they immediately recognised from his TV travel shows as his mother.

'I don't believe it!' said Matt, his eyes alighting on someone else. 'Over by the bar look, it's Nick Helm!'

Sure enough the grizzle-haired comic was standing at the bar, chatting to a blonde woman.

'Who's that with him?'

'It's only Sara Pascoe!' said Matt, shaking his head in wonder. He was a big fan of both of them.

'Let's go and get a selfie,' said Rob, starting towards them, but Matt held him back.

'Bit naff, isn't it?' he said, remembering how he used to feel shortly after his appearance on *The T Factor* when strangers came up to him and demanded selfies.

'Fair enough,' said Rob, having second thoughts – he could remember those times too. 'This looks like the place to be, doesn't it, Matt?' he said, looking around.

'Yup, and you'd get a lot of walk-up if you were doing your show at one of these venues.'

'We really need to go to some gigs,' said Matt with a sigh. 'We've been here over a week and we haven't seen a single stand-up!'

'Well, Mr G said he'd take us along to a show on

Saturday night, but I bet it's some play he's had his eye on,' said Rob, nodding in agreement.

'There's nothing for it, Roberto, we're going to have to escape,' said Matt with a cheeky grin.

'Escape? If we get caught we'll be murdered,' said Rob, but Matt could see he'd sparked his interest.

'What we need is a way of getting into the city centre . . .'

'Need a hand with that, Mr Brydon?' said Matt, sidling up to the old actor as he started setting up for his show that afternoon.

'Oh, thank you, Matt,' said Geraint Brydon, handing Matt a huge swan costume. 'That's very helpful.'

'Many in?' said Matt, forcing the thing through the narrow fire escape at the back of the metal container.

'Oh! Careful with that,' said Geraint taking it from him and placing it gently on the floor in the wings. 'My mother made it you know. From three feather pillows. I daresay it'll be another quiet one. To be honest I don't bother checking any more.

Numbers are down every year. It is what it is. There are no certainties if you choose to take the creative path. The triumph is in doing it at all.'

'You're absolutely right,' said Matt, nodding his head emphatically. 'Perhaps you should leaflet the queue for our show?'

'That's not a bad idea,' said Geraint brightly. 'That is if you and your friends don't mind?'

'I don't see why not,' said Matt. Then he paused as he prepared to ask the man the question he really wanted an answer to. 'Er . . . someone said you live in the city centre. Is that right?' he said, trying his best to make it sound like a casual enquiry.

'Yes, that's right, in my parents' flat. It's not ideal but it is nice and central. It's just a shame I can't afford to rent a venue in town too. It's all changed since the big promoters moved in. Everyone put their prices up and squeezed us little people out.'

'So you're going back there tonight then, after your show?' said Matt

'Yes, I'll go and have something in the canteen, read my book for a bit as I come down from the thrill of performance, then head home.'

'So . . . what time would you be heading off then?' said Matt nonchalantly.

'Oh, well, let me see, about six I suppose? Why?'

'Any chance of a lift?' said Matt.

After the show finished, Matt and Rob did their fair share of the tidying up, then went and found Miss Jolly.

'Miss Jolly?' said Matt, taking the lead.

'Yes, Matt, what's up?'

'Oh nothing's up, miss,' said Matt. 'Me and Rob have been invited to see the show after our one – you know, the play about Brexit?'

She nodded.

'Well, since doing the Shakespeare thing, both me and Rob have become really interested in drama, haven't we, Rob?'

'Er ... yes. Yes,' said Rob, shifting uneasily on the spot.

'So we were just checking that's OK?'

Miss Jolly looked a little surprised at the request but was happy to hear of Matt's enthusiasm for serious drama. 'But how would you get back to the hostel?' she said.

'Oh well, you know Mr Brydon? Well, he's staying to watch it too and has offered us a lift, so ...'

Miss Jolly took a few moments to weigh up her response and as she was doing so, who should walk past but Geraint Brydon. 'Ah, just the person,' she said, accosting him. 'Is it true you've offered these two a lift, Geraint?' she said.

Geraint squinted at them, then at her, then nodded his head. 'Yes, yes, not a problem, plenty of room in the car.'

Miss Jolly nodded her head. 'Thanks, that's much appreciated.'

'Not at all,' said Mr Brydon.

'So what are you going to do about dinner?' she said, turning back to the boys.

'Oh well, we'd just get something in the canteen.'

'And what time would you be back?' she said.

'Well, the play's quite a long one, then dinner . . . so, er . . . ten?'

'Ten?!' exclaimed Miss Jolly.

'Nine thirty?' said Matt, realising he was involved in a careful negotiation.

'Hmmmm,' she said, mulling it over. 'Right, well I s'pose that's fine. I'll see you back at the hostel.' She then turned and headed towards the minibus.

Once the minibus had pulled away and was out of

sight, Matt and Rob looked at each other and burst out laughing.

'Just one small thing,' said Rob. 'How *are* we going to get back?'

'Oh, let's worry about that when the time comes,' said Matt, looking at his phone. 'For now we've got exactly five hours of freedom.'

34
Full of Beans

For such an unassuming bloke, Geraint Brydon drove very fast indeed. In fact it was fair to say he drove like a complete lunatic. On the relatively short trip into the city centre he nearly ran over a woman with a pram on a zebra crossing and had countless near misses with other cars, including a huge articulated lorry at a T-junction. By the time he dropped the boys outside the Fringe Office they were both feeling quite sick.

'Thanks, Mr Brydon,' said Matt as he staggered out of the passenger seat.

'No problem! Have a great night and see you

tomorrow!' said Geraint brightly, completely unaware of the distress he'd caused. He honked his horn a couple of times and pulled away with a screech, nearly knocking a pizza delivery boy off his bike. As Matt saw this happen he reached into his pocket for his little black book.

'Uh-oh!' said Rob with a laugh. 'The comedy genius has had another idea!'

Matt grinned as he scribbled 'Pizza delivery boy knocked off bike' on one of the pages.

Though they'd both walked the Edinburgh streets a lot and got to know the town pretty well over the last nine days, they felt a thrill at being on their own and unsupervised.

They quickly found the Pleasance again and eagerly dodged through the huge stone archway. There was a chalkboard outside the box office, the sort you might see in a restaurant advertising the specials – only rather than food, this was a list of comedians and what time they were on. Matt looked at his watch.

'The Comedy Patch – what's that?' said Rob, scanning the list.

'Hmmm,' said Matt, looking around at the posters that were cramming every square inch of the walls and windows. 'Ah, here we are, look!' And he pointed to a big A2 poster with a photo of four young people on it under the heading 'The Comedy Patch'. There was a quote from a listing magazine that said 'Promising new comics – catch them before they're famous!'

'Looks like a stand-up show,' said Matt approvingly. 'Although I've not heard of any of the acts . . .'

'Wanna go for it?' said Rob. 'I mean, we haven't got long.'

'Let's do it!,' said Matt, and they joined the queue for the box office.

The show was in the Cabaret Bar venue at the top left of the Pleasance courtyard, and walking in immediately made Matt feel jealous. Compared to the metal box they were playing every night, this was like the London Palladium.

There was a low stage against one wall, surrounded by rows of raked seating and a fully functioning bar at the back of the room.

They took their seats and pretty soon the lights dimmed, the music got louder and a rotund bloke with a broad London accent burst through the curtains with a big 'please-like-me' smile.

'You may be able to tell from my accent that I'm from London!' he said, and there were a few groans from the sizeable Scottish contingent in the crowd.

'Yeah, all right, luv, it wasn't me that killed Braveheart,' he said, a reference to the old movie about the Scottish resistance fighter William Wallace.

He picked on a couple in the front row, who it turned out were from Norway and had a lot of fun playing with the stereotype of a marauding Viking.

'So have you pillaged any villages yet or are you waiting till it gets dark?' said the comic, to a sizeable laugh.

Matt looked across at Rob, who was chuckling

along, but he wasn't particularly impressed. He'd found that since becoming a comic himself he found it difficult to watch a comedian without analysing their act. He couldn't just appreciate it at face value like a regular punter would. He spent his time trying to second guess where their gags were going, or taking apart the nuts and bolts of their routines and comparing it to other acts he'd seen. After about ten minutes the audience were nicely warmed up and the MC returned the mic to its stand in preparation for bringing on the first act.

'Please give it up for John Beans!'

'John Beans, that's a good name,' chuckled Rob, but Matt didn't laugh along. He was always rather suspicious of acts with 'comedy' names.

A skinny man in his late twenties peered nervously out from the gap in the curtains. He had large black-framed glasses which were perched on a nose that seemed too big for his face. There were a few nervous titters as he popped his head back in behind the curtains like he was some sort of tortoise.

The audience waited, and slowly the face popped back out again – this time to a laugh. Then the comic slowly appeared from behind the curtains. He was wearing a sort of khaki suit with short sleeves, short trousers and white socks under sandals – never a particularly good look. The audience laughed heartily at the full picture. He gently tiptoed, painstakingly slowly, towards the mic, paused and then let out a loud burp.

He looked startled as if he hadn't been expecting it.

'Thanks very much, goodnight!' he said and made

to leave the stage – to a huge laugh and a round of applause. Matt was immediately pulled in – this was a true original. John Beans then fumbled with the microphone for what seemed like an age and each attempt to remove the microphone got bigger and bigger laughs. Finally he got the mic off the stand – which prompted another huge round of applause. 'Thank you!' said the young comic and promptly placed the microphone back in the stand to another big laugh and round of applause.

'That guy with the glasses was great, wasn't he?' said Matt as they wandered out into the courtyard after the show. All the comics on the bill had been good, but for Matt it was John Beans who was the star of the show. It was dark now and the place was illuminated only by strings of light bulbs strung around the four enclosing walls, which gave it a sort of magical quality. It was also heaving with people.

'We'd better get back!' said Rob, looking at his watch.

'He's there, look!' said Matt, pointing to a door round the back of the Cabaret Bar, where John Beans – now dressed more appropriately for the Edinburgh weather in a baseball cap and jeans and slightly more understated glasses – was emerging carrying a large sports bag.

'Let's go and say hello,' said Matt, walking towards the young comic, pushing his way through the hordes of people as he went. 'Excuse me, Mr Beans?' he said politely.

John Beans looked at him and took a moment to focus on the young boy in front of him.

'I . . . we . . . we really enjoyed your set,' Matt said, thrusting his hands in his pockets, realising he didn't really have much else to say.

'You're Matt Millz!' said John Beans, raising his eyebrows, his face breaking into one of the big smiles that had so charmed his audience.

Matt, of course, was thrilled. 'Yes! Yes that's right. You know me? I mean, you saw me on *The T Factor*?'

'Yeah, when was it? Last year sometime. Yes, it was really funny.'

Rob gave Matt a nudge. 'Oh, sorry! This is my mate Rob.'

'Hi,' said John Beans, shaking Rob's hand. He turned back to Matt. 'You're doing a show up here, aren't you?'

'Yes I am,' said Matt. 'Venue 44, Splashes Leisure Centre?'

'Oh, I don't know that one,' said John.

'It's a little bit off the beaten track,' said Matt. 'But it's a group show, a bit like yours.'

'Yes, I saw the names … Jamie someone on the list?'

'Castle,' said Rob. 'He's really good!'

John Beans nodded.

'The first week was pretty bad audience wise. We had to cancel the first night because no one turned up,' said Matt.

'Been there, done that, bought the T-shirt, worn the T-shirt, cut the T-shirt up and used it as a flag to attract attention when I was kidnapped!' joked John Beans. Matt and Rob laughed. 'There's just so many shows on it's virtually impossible to cut through the noise,' he said sagely. 'Anyway, I've got to get going,' he said. 'There's an open mic night across town and I've got a couple of gags I want to try out.'

Matt's ears pricked up. 'Open mic night?' he said.

'Yeah,' said John. 'You know, where comics try out stuff.' Then he looked at Matt. 'I'm sure you could get five minutes of stage time if you wanted. I mean, I know the girl who runs it . . .'

Matt's answer was immediate. 'Yup, up for that!' he said eagerly.

'Hang on!' said Rob, tapping his watch. 'We really need to be getting back, Matt. If we miss the last bus back to Dalkeith we're in big trouble!'

'Listen,' said Matt, taking him to one side. 'That's a detail.'

'Yeah, a very important detail. Mr G will kill us if we roll in late,' said Rob.

It was all very well wanting to try out some new

gags, but what exactly would he be getting out of it? Apart from a whole heap of trouble.

Matt hesitated. 'We'll make that last bus, trust me, Rob,' he said at last, making his mind up, and he followed John Beans out of the Pleasance courtyard.

35

Cellar Full of Noise

It was a ten-minute walk across town to a basement club called the Comedy Cellar where a lively crowd were gathered, sitting at tables as a motley procession of stand-up comics got up and tried out their stuff.

John Beans introduced Matt to the girl who was running the club. At first she was reluctant to let Matt and Rob in because of their age, but John explained about *The T Factor* and how Matt just wanted a little stage time. In the end she agreed, asking Matt to keep it to a 'tight five' and that she'd put him on after the next act. That didn't leave long for him to get his set together. He hadn't come prepared to do a gig, but luckily he had his trusty little black book in his pocket, so he went off into a corner by himself and flicked through it for some ideas.

In no time the guy on stage had finished up to a few claps, and the MC was back and announcing Matt. There was a general hubbub of surprise as Matt took the stage – mainly at his age, but a few of the punters clearly recognised him from TV.

'Hi!' said Matt, looking around the subterranean room – the low light and general lack of fresh air seemed to have rendered the audience semi-comatose. 'I can't stay long because my mum's coming to pick me up,' he said, which got a reasonable laugh – it was a line that Matt had used before.

'So . . .' he said, and launched into one of his new bits. 'My dad got some of that new-car-smell spray – you know, the stuff that's supposed to make your car smell like a new car?'

The audience made a few noises, a few disinterested grunts.

'Yeah, so he sprayed this stuff around the car – it's

an old car, and it did end up smelling like a brand-new car . . .'

'So what?' came a heckle from the back.

'First, thanks for your interest, sir,' said Matt, quick as a flash. 'And secondly, he managed to sell the car to a partially sighted man . . . who thought it was a new car!' There was a laugh. Matt nodded, smiling, visibly pleased with himself. 'The guide dog was on to him though.'

Another laugh.

'Yeah, the guide dog was pawing him saying, "Don't buy it! Don't buy it!"' he said, dropping to one knee and doing his best dog impression.

Another big laugh.

He looked down at the back of his hand and saw the words 'Pizza Delivery Boy', and a tiny voice inside him yelled, 'Go for it!' And although he had no real idea of how the routine might work, off he went. 'My dad knocked a pizza delivery boy off his bike the other day,' he said, nodding. 'Yeah he felt really bad about it . . . he felt bad for knocking him off and *I* felt bad for eating the pizza! Well, we were waiting so long for the ambulance to turn up and I was starving!'

The new routine got massive laughs. Matt looked over at Rob leaning against the wall near the back of the room, taking photos with his phone. Rob grinned and nodded. They both knew where the idea had come from and how fresh it was. After his experience at the Comedy Store though, Matt was in no mood to overstay his welcome – besides, they had to get that last bus.

'Hey, you know when you first get on a bus and you're walking up the bus but the bus is going forward, so technically that first few moments of the journey you're standing still? I think you shouldn't have to pay for that part of the journey. Why should you have to pay when you're not going anywhere?' There was no laugh. Even though it sounded like a gag from the way Matt had set it up, the punchline didn't quite cut it.

He felt a slight feeling of panic as his brain whirred through the options – he could get off, but to no laugh (not really an option), he could risk trying another new gag, or he could sign off with one of his 'bankers', a gag he knew always killed.

His ego got the better of him and he flashed an apologetic look at Rob as he heard himself say, 'You probably noticed that I'm pretty young for a comic . . . in fact, I'm so young that when I have a drink I like to have a rusk with it!'

He finally got the laugh he was looking for, jumped down off the stage and headed for the exit where Rob was waiting.

'Hey, Matt! Nice one!' It was John Beans.

'Cheers, John! Thanks for giving me a chance!'

'We'd better get a move on if we're going to make that bus,' said Rob anxiously.

'See you around, Matt, and good luck,' said John as the boys headed up the stairs towards the exit.

They came out of the club to street level and immediately tried to get their bearings.

'Now where?' said Matt.

'Er . . .' Rob took out his phone and studied the map. 'I think it's left. No, hang on . . .' he said, turning his phone upside down. 'No, right . . . No, hang on . . .'

Just then Matt heard his name being called.

'Matt Mills!'

It was a voice he recognised. He looked across the road to see Mr Gillingham leaning out of the window of their minibus. He didn't look very happy.

'Get in! Now!' growled the teacher. Matt had never seen him so angry. Matt looked at Rob, Rob gulped hard.

'Uh-oh, game's up,' muttered Matt out of the corner of his mouth as they walked towards the minibus.

Mr Gillingham didn't say anything until they'd got out of the city centre – it was as if he was too furious to speak, but as they hit the ring road he let rip.

'Can you imagine the trouble we'd get into if something happened to you?!' he snapped, clearly trying to keep a lid on his emotions. The boys stared silently at their feet. 'Well? Do you?' said Mr G almost shouting.

'No, sir,' said Matt.

'Well, we'd be in serious trouble and would probably lose our jobs!' said Mr G.

'It was my fault,' said Matt. 'It was all my idea.'

'I don't doubt it, but the fact is that Robert here went along with it.'

'How did you ... find out where we were?' said Matt weakly.

'Well, when you weren't back when you said you would be and didn't answer your phones, we started to panic. Fortunately Ahmed was keeping an eye on your Instagram account and saw Rob's pictures of the club.'

'Oh, I'm really sorry, sir,' said Matt, and he meant it; the last thing he wanted was for Mr Gillingham to get into trouble.

'Bit late for that. You think I want to be driving round in the middle of the night in the pitch-black looking for you two?'

'No, sir,' they said in unison.

'No, no I don't.' He drove on some more in silence. Then after a while he said, 'Anyway, how'd it go?' turning to them with a smile.

'What, sir?' said Matt.

'How'd the gig go? Get much new stuff?'

'He did brilliantly, sir,' said Rob, brightening. 'He even made up a joke on the spot!'

'Hmmm. So it was worth it then . . . ?' said Mr G.

'Er . . . well . . .' Matt hesitated. 'That depends, sir,' he said a little tentatively, 'on what you're going to do with us.'

'I should send you home, that's what I should do,' said the teacher.

Matt let out a long groan. 'Please don't do that, sir,' he said with genuine despair in his voice.

'That's what I *should* do,' said Mr G.

Matt exchanged a pained look with Rob.

'But since the gig went well, I'm not going to do that.'

Matt and Rob let out a huge sigh of relief. 'No, I want you to do all the washing-up after breakfast and dinner for the rest of the trip,' said Mr Gillingham, looking at them with a big smile on his face.

'Yes, sir, no problem! We'll have those plates gleaming, sir,' said Matt.

'But if it happens again,' said Mr G, suddenly turning serious, 'you'll be back in Kent so fast your feet won't touch the ground, and you can forget the idea of any other school trips.'

'Yes, sir,' they said.

As the minibus pulled up outside the hostel a worried-looking Miss Jolly was standing waiting by the door.

'And, sir?' said Matt

'Yes?' said Mr G, yanking on the handbrake.

'Thanks for the lift.'

'Huh!' grunted Mr Gillingham.

'I found them!' he said to Miss Jolly as he climbed down from the bus.

Miss Jolly shook her head. 'Oh, Paul, where were they?' she said. Matt immediately felt very guilty – it looked like she'd been crying.

'Sorry, miss,' he said.

'I'll tell you later,' said Mr Gillingham, rolling his eyes to the heavens. Then he turned to the boys. 'Now get to bed and try not to wake the others.' And they hurried into the warm hostel.

Matt looked at his watch. It was almost midnight – what an adventure!

36
And the Nominations Are...

Kitty had been right about the new shape of the show. It gave Matt a much easier time and also a chance to have a look at his list for new ideas before going on between the other acts. There'd been an unexpected boost to ticket sales for *Othello*, which looked like it was heading for a sell-out too.

'At this rate, we're going to go home with some dosh in our pockets,' said Ahmed with a broad grin as they gathered round their usual table in the canteen for their post-show snack.

'Hang on, where's Kit?' said Alex, putting her

hands over the bowl of chips to prevent the boys from helping themselves.

Just then, Matt's phone buzzed into life. It was Kitty and she sounded very excited indeed.

'Matt! Is Jamie with you?' she said.

'Yes ...' said Matt suspiciously. 'We're all here, where are you? The chips are getting cold!'

'Put me on speakerphone,' she said. Matt did as he was told and indicated to the others to lean in.

'Come on then, Kit. Spill the beans, what's got you all excited?' asked Matt.

'The show's been nominated!' she screeched.

'Nominated? What, you mean for a—?' said Matt.

'For a Wetfizz award! Well, not the main one, but for the best newcomer! It's fantastic news!'

At the other end of the line Kitty Hope heard a clunk as Matt dropped the phone. That noise was followed by the distant sound of young people celebrating.

'He looks like a judge,' said Matt peering round the curtain before the show the next day.

Kitty had explained that after the nominations for the Wetfizz Awards were announced, the five judges would go back and watch the nominated shows over the  ensuing days – then the winners would be announced at midnight on Saturday, the last Saturday of their run.

'She could be a judge,' said Alex leaning in next to him. 'She's got a piece of paper and a pen!'

Matt nodded. He'd been really impressed with how Alex had turned her luck around. She'd really worked hard on her act, and with Matt's help had refined it to a really tight little set – there were still a couple of dud gags but her kooky charm and the accuracy of her impressions somehow managed to get her through.

'Try not to let it affect the show,' said Kitty, joining them backstage. 'Remember, it's the whole audience you're entertaining, not just one or two people who may or may not be judges.'

The show went really well again, albeit not quite as well as the night before.

'Wednesday night,' said Matt knowingly. 'Mainly smilers, you see – they're all thinking about work tomorrow.'

'Oh, Jamie,' said Kitty, coming to join them. 'I've had some good news for you. That woman with the pen and paper – she wasn't a judge, she's a radio producer. She's putting together a sort of 'Best of the Fringe' showcase for Radio 2 – and she wants you to be on it!'

'Oh,' said Jamie, looking far from pleased.

'It's good news, Jamie, what's up?' said Kit.

'Oh, er . . . nothing . . . er, I . . . yeah, fine whatever you think. Sorry, I guess it just made me feel a bit nervous – I've never done anything like that before,' he said.

'Well, get used to it. I'm pretty sure it's going to be the first of many!'

'Er . . . was it just Jamie, or is this producer lady interested in anyone else from the show?' said Matt a little disconcerted.

'Sorry, Matt, it's just Jamie they're interested in,' said Kitty apologetically.

'Oh,' said Matt. 'I thought that ...'

'Yes, I know, I did suggest you do the show too but she said they couldn't really have more than one act from the same show and that some people would already know you from *The T Factor* – the thing with these people is they're always after finding someone or something new.'

'Jeez!' exclaimed Matt. 'I still feel pretty new!'

'I know, I know ...' she said, putting a comforting hand on his shoulder. 'But Jamie being on that programme is not just good for him, it's good for the show too.'

'True,' said Matt, and then he turned to Jamie. 'Nice one, mate, you deserve it,' he said, shaking his hand.

'So tomorrow morning, let's go through your set list and work out which five minutes you're going to do,' said Kitty to Jamie, who had suddenly turned as white as a sheet.

37
Return of a National Treasure

'Weird about Jamie. Anyone else would have been thrilled to be offered a five-minute spot on a national radio station,' said Matt to Rob a little later as they were packing away the set. 'But he looked like it was the last thing on earth he wanted to do.'

Suddenly there was a loud bang that sounded like a gun going off. 'Get on the floor!' screamed Ahmed. 'It's a terrorist attack!'

Matt looked to where the noise had come from and could see a strange figure in a motorcycle helmet careering across the car park on a battered old motorbike, smoke pouring out of the exhaust pipe, and every few yards there was a loud pop as the engine backfired.

'Woooooah!' came a voice from inside the helmet. A voice that Matt was pretty sure he recognised. The bike wove erratically, narrowly missing a couple of cars. It then appeared to accelerate towards the metal container.

'Look out!' shouted Matt and managed to grab Alex and push her out of the way as the bike crashed into Jamie's dad's inflatable house. There was a loud pop and a hissing sound as the house gradually deflated.

The rider of the bike appeared from amongst the torn fabric and struggled to pull off his helmet. Matt stepped forward to help. He knew who was under it before the helmet came off.

'I must get the brakes fixed on that thing,' the rider said, looking down at the dented frame of his motor scooter – it was Bobby Bath.

'Bobby!' exclaimed Matt, and flung his arms round his old friend. 'What are you doing here?'

'Yes, well, you didn't think I'd miss your Edinburgh debut, did you?' said Bobby, his face lighting up into a huge smile. 'Well, I say that, but my trip's a bit of business as well as pleasure – they've got me hosting this gala night at the Playhouse. I'm introducing the best of the Fringe apparently, although I'm not sure why I'm doing it – I'm not really an MC.'

'Tell me about it,' said Matt ruefully.

'It's cos you're a national treasure, Bobby,' said Rob, lifting the bike away from the wreckage of the inflatable house.

'Yes, well, I'm not sure about that,' said Bobby modestly. 'Although if I'd known the amount of work I'd get from having a heart attack I'd have had one sooner!'

'Don't, Bobby,' said Kitty, looking worried. 'How is everything, health wise?'

'Well, the docs have told me to take it easy, but I sort of know my limitations now. My days of two-hour shows are over, but that doesn't mean I can't still have some fun. More importantly, how's your show been going? That review in the paper was fan-blooming-tastic! You couldn't have written a better one yourselves. And this new kid – this Jamie – sounds like a real find, Kitty!'

'He's doing really well ...' said Kitty, nodding and looking at Matt for his reaction; she still felt a little bit like she'd betrayed Matt in some way by promoting Jamie to the top of the bill.

At that moment, who should wander up but Jamie. 'What's happened to Dad's house?' he said, looking gobsmacked.

'It got demolished,' laughed Ahmed.

'He's going to be furious when he sees that! He's coming up tomorrow.'

'Oops!' said Matt. 'But Jamie, there's someone I'd

like you to meet. Bobby? This is Jamie Castle.'

'Always happy to meet another fellow comic,' said Bobby, shaking the boy's hand. 'And sorry about your dad's, er . . . house.'

'Looks more like a bungalow now,' joked Matt.

'Yes, well I'm happy to pay for . . . er . . . a puncture repair outfit!' Bobby started laughing too but Jamie didn't see the funny side.

'You don't know what he's like . . .' he said anxiously.

'We'll fix it up,' said Matt reassuringly, realising that Jamie was genuinely worried.

'Yeah, it looks worse than it is – it's just a small tear. We can sort that out, no probs,' said Ahmed, inspecting the damage.

'So where's the venue?'

'That's the venue,' laughed Alex pointing at the metal box.

'It must be like a tin of sardines when it's full,' said Bobby, a look of wonder on his face.

'That's good,' said Matt, reaching for his little black book. 'Can I have that?'

'Of course! Good to see you're still adding new stuff into the act, even at this late stage,' said Bobby admiringly.

'Oh, Bobby, it's been great for material. I've got so much new stuff!'

'Shall we go and get a cup of tea?' said Bobby. Matt nodded and the two of them wandered towards the Leisure Centre deep in conversation.

They made an unlikely couple as they walked into the Splashes canteen. Matt got a bottle of Coke and Bobby got a big mug of tea and some shortbread.

'It's not particularly short, is it?' said Bobby.

'Well, it's shorter than a French stick!' laughed Matt.

'So come on then,' said Bobby, taking a sip from his mug of tea. 'Tell me all about it.'

Matt told Bobby the whole story: how they'd struggled to find an audience, but how the video of him and Rob being threatened by Dickie Hart had gone viral and drawn a crowd; how Jamie had turned up with a rock-solid fifteen minutes that always killed; and how Matt had found it difficult to follow him, and had been pushed back in the bill and become the MC with Jamie being the headliner.

'Hmm, well I can't wait to see him,' said Bobby, taking another sip of tea. 'So how do you feel about him? I mean, it must have made you pretty fed up – it's never nice to have someone come along and get all the attention . . .' Bobby was right; he knew instinctively how the comedian's mind worked. 'I remember that feeling, when one minute you're the centre of attention, the one who everyone wants to know, then it's someone else. There's always someone snapping at your heels in this business. You just have to treat it like a game because if you let it get to you it leads to bitterness – never very attractive. The way I see it, if Jamie's pulling in the punters then it's all to the good – more people are getting to see you and Alex and Neil. It's good news.'

'Yeah, it was pretty bad at first but I'm dealing with it,' said Matt matter-of-factly. 'In some ways it's made my job easier, taken the pressure off . . . It's meant I can muck about more, so I've had a much bigger turnover of gags than Jamie. He's stuck with the exact same fifteen.'

'Ah well, he feels under pressure to deliver – we've all had that feeling,' said Bobby.

'Now, yes, but he stuck to the same act even when we were getting only a few people in,' said Matt with a frown. 'That's what I don't get about him, Bobby. Don't get me wrong, his act's really funny – as you'll find out – but he doesn't have the interest in gags and routines, about what makes people laugh like we do, you know?'

'Yeah? Well, we're all different, I guess,' said Bobby, looking at his watch. 'Anyway, that's enough yackin'. You better join your mates for some chips!' He pointed to a table across the canteen where the others were sitting. Bobby drained the last dregs of tea from his mug and stood up. 'See you tomorrow night. I'll be at the show – if I can get a ticket!'

38

The Hare and the Tortoise

As Matt came off after the stand-up show the following afternoon, Bobby was waiting for him with a big grin on his face.

'That was knockout!' he said, putting an arm round Matt in a sort of half hug. 'Loved the stuff about the pizza delivery boy!'

'That was new tonight,' said Matt excitedly, his face flushed from the buzz of doing the show.

'Put it there!' said Bobby, shaking Matt's hand. 'I tell you what you could do, you could add a bit to it – something about still being hungry and looking for another delivery boy to knock off?'

'Ha! That's good,' said Matt, reaching for his little black book.

'Hi, Bobby. I hope you enjoyed the show,' It was Jamie, and he was with his parents.

'I did, Jamie, I really enjoyed it – everyone was great,' he said, choosing his words carefully. 'Neil's really come on since I last saw him – and Alex has got really good.'

'Yes, but the real star is my boy,' said Ted Castle, patting Jamie on the head. Jamie squirmed and pulled away from his dad.

'Yes, well, it's a team effort, but of course, yes, you went over really well, Jamie,' said Bobby, a little disconcerted by Ted Castle's bluntness. 'Did you enjoy it?'

'Yeah, yeah,' said Jamie, nodding. 'It was a good crowd. What did you think of the play though, *Othello*?'

'Bit over my head, son,' said Bobby. 'But I could see you were really into it. There's just so much talent on that stage!'

'I'm into acting more than I am the comedy really,' said Jamie brightly.

'As a hobby,' interjected Ted. 'There's enough actors in the world. The chances of you making the big time are miniscule. No, better to get a proper profession under your belt.'

'Someone's got to make it,' said Bobby. Matt nodded in agreement. Jamie looked at his dad hopefully, but Ted Castle wasn't laughing.

'Actors are two a penny. Like I say, it's good to have a hobby, as long as it doesn't interfere with the schoolwork,' he said, then something caught his eye and he wandered off.

'As you can see, Dad's not convinced,' said Jamie with a resigned sigh.

'Jamie,' came a voice from the front of the container. They looked round to see Ted Castle with a face like thunder inspecting his inflatable house.

'Ooops! Looks like Dad's spotted the damage. I'd better go. . .'

'I'll come too,' said Bobby. 'It was me that caused

it, it's only right I should take the blame. I'll catch
you up,' he said to Matt.

'What did you really think of Jamie's act?' said
Matt as they walked across the car park later to
the minibus.

'I liked it,' said Bobby. 'It's hard not to, but he's
not really a comic.'

'What do you mean?' said Matt.

'Well, he's saying funny stuff, but he's not funny
in himself,' said Bobby. Then he stopped and turned
to Matt. 'Listen, son, you shouldn't worry about
what Jamie's doing. You have to give the crowd
what *you* want to give them, otherwise you're just a
crowd-pleaser.'

'But he was that good from the word "go", Bobby,' said Matt. 'And it's exactly the same, word for word every night!'

'Well, that's fine. What Jamie does is up to Jamie. You, you're different, you're on a journey. You're – without getting too lah-di-dah or, what do you call it, pretentious, about it – you're trying to push it, to find out new ways to make people laugh. You're interested in, I don't know what you might call it, the form of it! Yes, Jamie's going down better than you at the moment, but it's like he's come to the end of his journey – he's arrived at what he wants to do. But you, you're still on yours and I'd bet my motor scooter that at the end of your journey, you'll be at a much more interesting place. It's like that story about the hare and the tortoise.'

'A hare and a tortoise?' said Matt, looking slightly perplexed.

'Yeah, there's this hare and it's having a race with a tortoise—' said Bobby

'Why?' said Matt.

'Eh?' said Bobby.

'Why would a hare be racing a tortoise?'

'Um . . . dunno, ha! It's a just a story, one of those fable things. Anyway, to cut a long story short, the hare sets off and takes the lead early on but the tortoise wins in the end,' said Bobby.

'How?' said Matt.

'I can't remember! Look, never mind!' said Bobby, stopping to catch his breath. He suddenly looked all of his eighty-three years. 'But take it from someone who knows. Forget Jamie. Try to enjoy his success. You'll be fine. It's the hare and the tortoise.'

39
Clean Underpants

As the minibus pulled into the car park, Matt could see the familiar shape of the Astra, and leaning on the bonnet were his mum and Ian. As soon as Mr G had parked up, Matt was out of the door and running to meet them.

'Oh, my poor little boy! You look terrible!' shrieked his mum, sweeping him up into her arms. 'You look like you've lost weight! Have they not been feeding you properly?!'

'I've only been away for two weeks,' said Matt, struggling to escape from her grasp.

'You look like a skeleton!' she said melodramatically.

'Now I've brought you some clean underpants,' she said, producing a Marks and Spencer's carrier bag from inside her coat.

'Mum!' said Matt, snatching the bag and stuffing it under his jacket.

'All right, Matt?' said Ian, putting a paternal hand on Matt's shoulder. 'Your mum's missed you, you know.'

'So I see,' said Matt

'How's it been going?'

'Bit of a shaky start, but the last week has been knockout!' said Matt.

'Good, I'm pleased for you. I'm glad the gamble's paid off,' said Ian with a satisfied smile. 'Obviously we're coming to the Shakespeare thing, then staying for the stand-up show, then after that I thought maybe we could take you and a friend out for a pizza. How's that sound?'

'That sounds very, very good,' said Matt.

Three hours later Ian and Matt's mum emerged

blinking from the metal container. 'That was great, Matt,' said Ian.

'I am *so* proud of you,' shrilled his mum.

'Well, it's a group effort . . .' said Matt modestly.

'I know, but even so,' said Ian. 'I was surprised at how good the Castle boy was – seems like a natural,' he added.

'Yeah, yeah, he always smashes it,' said Matt.

'Where's your friend?' said Ian

'Oh, on their way,' said Matt.

'Well, he'd better get a move on, the table's booked for seven thirty and the traffic into the city is appalling.'

'Actually it's not a he,' said Matt sheepishly. 'It's a she. Say hello to Alex . . .'

'Hi,' said Alex as she joined Matt. 'Matt's told me a lot about you.'

Ian turned to his wife and exchanged a knowing look. 'I wish I could say he'd done the same about you!' Then he stepped forward and shook her hand.

*

'I can't believe it's our last show tomorrow night,' said Alex as they tucked into their pizza.

'Are you planning a party?' said Matt's mum. 'Or something to celebrate?'

'Mr G said he's booked tickets for a show, but he hasn't told us which one,' said Alex.

'I bet it's some boring Shakespeare thing that's three hours long,' said Matt.

'Yes, but at least he's said we can stay up to find out who's won.'

'Ah yes,' said Ian. 'The famous Wetfizz Awards. Well, if it was up to me, you'd win it ten times over, Matt. And even if you don't you've sort of won anyway.'

'Amen to that!' said Matt's mum, holding her glass of white wine aloft. 'To *Matt Millz and Friends*!' she said, and they all clinked glasses.

40
Their Last Saturday

Before their final show, Mr Gillingham called them all into the metal container. He stood on the stage as they sat in the rows of plastic chairs like they were his audience.

'I just wanted to say a few words about the trip before we all get preoccupied with packing up and getting ready to go home tomorrow,' he said. 'And what I wanted to say was how proud I've been of what you've achieved.' As he spoke, Matt noticed a tear forming in his teacher's eye. 'You've turned out something really flippin' special here over these last two weeks, and you should really give yourselves a pat on the back.'

Matt giggled and immediately started patting Rob on the back and Rob then started patting Matt on the back.

'Yes, thank you, boys,' said Mr G, and Matt and Rob stopped mucking about and faced the front as he continued with his speech.

'I'm sure you'd all like to join me in thanking Stephanie – I mean Miss Jolly – for putting in so much hard work organising the trip to make sure it was the success that it's turned out to be.'

They all broke out into an enthusiastic round of applause as Miss Jolly joined Mr G on the stage and one of the younger girls presented her with a bunch of flowers.

'Actually, while we're on the subject of Miss Jolly, there is one more thing I'd like to say to her . . .' He turned to face her and fumbled in his pocket for something. He produced what looked like a small black box. There was a gasp from the girls as he suddenly descended on to one knee and cleared his throat to speak. 'Stephanie,' he said, 'will you marry me?' He then lifted the lid of the box to reveal a sparkly engagement ring.

Miss Jolly took a step back and her eyes filled with tears. 'Yes!' she said without a moment's hesitation. 'Yes! Of course I'll marry you!' she said, then she leaned down and gave Mr Gillingham a big kiss on the lips.

'Yaaaaaaaaay!' cheered the audience of kids jumping up and giving the couple a round of applause.

Thinking quickly, Ahmed pulled out his phone and started playing 'Marry You' by Bruno Mars and they all jumped around dancing. Eventually Mr Gillingham wiped his eyes and calmed everyone down.

'Right,' he said. 'I guess you want to know what we're going to see after the show tonight?'

There was a bit of chatter as the kids discussed what they thought it might be.

'Well, to celebrate the success of the play . . .'

'Here we go,' said Ahmed. 'Bet it's Shakespeare.'

'But also to celebrate the huge achievements of

Jamie, Matt, Alex and Neil, not to mention Kitty and Ahmed—'

'Ahem!' coughed Rob.

'Oh yes, and Rob of course for the poster.'

Rob stood up and took a bow.

'I've got us all tickets to the comedy gala at the Playhouse, featuring none other than Bobby Bath!'

'Yes!' shouted Matt, jumping to his feet, and they all started dancing again.

41

Badass

'Oh, look, Jamie's left his bag,' said Rob as they started loading out the set and props after the play, ready for their last stand-up gig of the run. Just as they spoke there was a *ping*! from inside the bag.

'Oh, sounds like he's left his phone in there,' said Ahmed.

'Bit careless, lads,' said Rob, unzipping the bag and reaching in. 'Let's see what he's got on it, shall we?'

'I don't think we should, Rob. I mean, there might be personal stuff . . .' said Matt.

'That's what I'm hoping,' replied Rob with a grin, fishing out the shiny top-of-the range iPhone.

'I really don't think—' said Matt, reaching forward to try and grab the phone off him.

'Oh. It's locked. Bang goes my bit of fun!' said Rob.

'Give it here,' said Ahmed, nonchalantly taking the phone from Rob's open palm. 'Let me just . . .' As he spoke his thumbs flicked up and down and back and forth across the screen until finally there was a soft click as the phone unlocked. 'There you go,' he said, handing it back to Rob. 'One open phone.'

'Wow!' said Rob. 'How'd you do that?'

'Well, there's some codes that everyone uses, stupidly. Jamie made the mistake of using 'password', only spelt P455w0rd. Pretty lame.'

Rob pressed the home button. 'Let's just have a quick look at his photos!' Matt tutted and rolled his eyes, but curiosity got the better of him and he sidled in a little closer so he could see over Rob's shoulder, reasoning with himself that it was only human nature to be interested.

'Ha! Look at the size of that Christmas turkey!' said Rob, flicking through some of Jamie's Christmas pics.

'Er, I think that's his younger brother having his nappy changed,' said Matt with a laugh.

'Any of his mum on the beach?' asked Ahmed with a sly smile.

'Ahmed!'

'What? She's fit!' he protested.

'What's he listening to?' said Rob. 'I bet it's Christine Aguilera or some lame brain rubbish.'

Rob clicked on Jamie's music app and the last thing Jamie had been listening to popped up. The three of them crowded round to read it.

'"Stand-up Live from the Cape Town Comedy Bunker!"' said Matt. 'What's that?'

'Only one way to find out!' said Rob, pressing play.

What the three boys heard next left them completely nonplussed. First was the rough atmosphere of a comedy club, some general chit-chat and audience hubbub, then some music followed by an announcer introducing the first act.

'*Ladies and gentlemen, please welcome your first act . . . Steve Kibuuka!*'

They heard a round of enthusiastic applause, then came a line that chilled Matt and the others to the bone.

'*Hey! Thanks for waiting! Great to be here! Hey, who's got a cat here?*' Matt, Rob and Ahmed looked at each other in amazement.

'That's Jamie's opening line,' said Rob. Then they listened some more.

'*You, madam, do you have a cat? No? But tell me, do you like cats?*'

'*Yes!*' came a distant voice from the audience

'*So get a cat! Is that so hard?*'

The audience on the audio dissolved into gales of laughter.

'*So what else do you like that you haven't got?*' said Steve Kibuuka.

'He's nicked his whole act from a South African comic,' said Ahmed shaking his head.

'He's certainly nicked one or two gags,' said Matt, defending his friend. But as the track played on, it became clear that Jamie hadn't just stolen one or two gags from this unknown South African comedian's set, he'd stolen virtually every single gag, word for word. And not just from him but from all four of the acts on the recording!

'I knew it!' said Matt, shaking his head. 'No wonder he never changed a single word of it, he couldn't! He was stuck with what he'd learned from this set!' He didn't feel pleased to discover that Jamie was a fraud, he actually felt a bit sick. Here was someone they'd all counted as a friend, deceiving them just to be a star.

'What do we do?' said Rob, slightly dizzy with the horror of the situation.

'We dump him in it,' said Ahmed coldly. 'You don't nick gags, right? We know that much.'

'Wait, let's think about this,' said Matt, trying to keep a cool head. 'What do we do? Er . . . we . . .'

'We dump him in it, simple as,' repeated Ahmed. 'He's a thief. How would those comedians in South Africa feel if they knew he was going around doing their stuff and passing it off as his own?'

'Yeah, and don't forget the show's up for that award. If the judges find out, it's bound to get us disqualified,' added Rob.

Matt ran his hand through his quiff. 'That's why he was so reluctant to do the radio spot – he knows there's a chance he may get found out. How did he think he was going to get away with it? I mean, if we hadn't sussed him out, someone else would have.'

'I bet that recording is on YouTube,' said Ahmed, grabbing the phone from the table. Pretty soon his flying thumbs had tracked down not just the audio, but a video of the whole night.

'He thought because they were based all those miles away he was safe. But these days everything is available to everybody, everything's just a couple of clicks away, if you know where to look.'

'What are the options?' said Matt, sitting down in the front row and taking out his little black book, opening it at a blank page. The others hopped down from the stage to join him as he scribbled 'Options' then underlined it twice.

'One – do nothing. We probably won't win best newcomer, no harm done, well, not much anyway.'

'No way,' said Ahmed, slapping his hand into his fist defiantly. 'That just ain't right. He needs to know we found him out and he hasn't got away with it.'

'I'm with Ahmed,' said Rob. 'I mean, I like the guy, but he lied to us.'

'OK, that's option one out. Option two – confront him.'

'Mega embarrassing,' groaned Ahmed with a whimper.

'Yeah,' agreed Rob. 'Bagsy not me doing it.'

'Then what?' said Matt, drawing an arrow from 'Confront him' leading to an empty box in which he drew a question mark. 'If he admits it and pulls out of the show, that leaves us a comic down for the last show . . .'

'Yeah, but if he gets found out it means a whole load of doo-doo all over us and the school and . . .' said Ahmed.

'Hmmmm.'

'He's got to pull out anyway,' said Ahmed. 'Unless he can come up with his own act.'

'How 'bout we tell his dad?' said Rob.

'Don't forget his dad paid for this whole trip,' said Ahmed. 'What if he pulls the plug on us, and makes us stump up the cost? Forget that!'

'OK,' said Matt, scribbling a number four. 'Er . . . what's number four?'

'There isn't one,' came a voice from behind them.

Matt spun round. 'Ian!'

'Yes.'

'How did you . . . ?'

'I thought Jamie's sudden comic abilities were a bit fishy, so I did a bit of digging myself. Ted mentioned that he used to go along to a comedy club in Cape Town and so last night when I got back to the hotel I googled it. Well, it didn't take me long to turn up that video. I arranged to meet Ted here to have a chat about it. See if there's some way we can fix it between us without too much fuss.'

Ahmed took a sharp intake of breath. 'Rather you than me, Mr W.'

Just then the door opened and in walked Ted Castle.

'Hi, Ian. Hi, fellas, how's it going? Any sign of Jamie? I texted him but he hasn't answered,' he said, completely oblivious to the drama soon to unfold.

'Hi, Ted, he hasn't answered because the boys here have got his phone,' said Ian with a very serious face.

'He left it behind,' added Matt nervously.

'Oh, that explains it. Give it here and I'll give it to him when I see him,' said Ted Castle, reaching out his hand for the phone. 'He really does need to look after his things better. That phone cost me a fortune, top of the range,' he said.

Matt, Rob and Ahmed all looked at each other nervously.

'Ted, I need to have a word,' said Ian.

'Sure, that's why I'm here. What's up? I really don't understand why we couldn't have chatted over the phone. I've got tickets for the ballet for the wife so I can't hang about—'

'There's something you should know about Jamie,' Ian broke in abruptly.

'What? What is it? You've found something on his phone?'

'You could say that,' muttered Ahmed under his breath. The whole situation was becoming very uncomfortable.

'He's a young boy, he's bound to have the odd dodgy photo,' said his dad with a chuckle.

'No,' said Ian forcefully. 'It's not a dodgy photo, Ted. I'm afraid Jamie has been cheating.'

'Cheating? What do you mean cheating? Cheating at what?'

'His comedy routine, the one that's been storming it every night here at the Edinburgh Festival – he stole it from a whole bunch of South African comics. After you mentioned the club last night, I googled it and there's a live recording and it's got all Jamie's jokes on it, only they're not Jamie's, are they?'

Ted Castle paused for a moment, then he quietly gave Ian his response. 'Well,' he said, fixing Ian squarely in the eye, 'all comedians borrow each other's gags, don't they? No real harm done.'

Matt gasped. 'You *knew*,' he whispered, then he spoke up. 'No they don't!' Matt stared at the stage, avoiding Mr Castle's gaze. 'That's just it, comics don't steal each other's material – that was in the bad old days.'

'Matt's right, it's not the seventies any more,' agreed Ian. 'A comic's act is their livelihood, Ted – as a businessman you'll understand that. Besides, as part of the show, Jamie's up for the newcomer award – what if they win it? There'll be a lot of press attention and someone is bound to put two and two together; then he'll be in all sorts of bother, and they'll all be dragged through the mud. It's not fair on Matt and the others – or, frankly, the school.'

'I'm willing to take that chance,' snapped Ted with a coldness in his voice. 'Give me the phone and not a word of this to anyone!'

'Well, you can have the phone, obviously,' said Ian, looking round at the other boys. 'But if you don't talk to him about this, I will, and if he doesn't drop out of the show I'm afraid I'll have to tell the organisers of the award. Sorry, Ted, but it's just not the way we do things over here.'

'Over here?' said Ted, his face reddening. 'Over here? You Brits really think you're something special, don't you? That you're a cut above, with your table manners and your afternoon tea and your royal family of weird inbred losers. May I remind you that I'm paying for this little shenanigan?'

'Well, I appreciate that,' said Ian, standing his ground, 'and I can see it's a really difficult position for you to be in, but we have to do the right thing here.'

'Do the right thing?' said Ted angrily raising his

voice. 'Yeah, you will do the right thing. You work for me, Woodward. The "right thing" as you call it is what I tell you to do. And I'm telling you, all of you –' he looked round at the other boys – 'to shut your faces!' He stepped forward so his nose was just a matter of centimetres from Ian's and lowered his voice to a half whisper. 'That's if you want to hang on to your job,' he snarled. With that, he snatched the phone from Ahmed, turned and marched off.

Rob let out a whistle of surprise.

'Wow!' said Matt, sitting back in his chair.

'That is one badass dude,' said Ahmed.

Ian was lost for words, staring into the middle distance, but after a few moments a determined look settled on his face.

42

A Slightly Shorter Show Than Planned

'We can't say anything or my stepdad gets the sack,' whispered Matt as they stood in the wings waiting to go on. They'd agreed not to tell Alex, Neil or Kitty about 'The Jamie Situation' but still hadn't worked out what to do about it.

It wasn't until Alex was onstage that Jamie reappeared.

'Hi, guys, how's it looking?' he said, stepping through the emergency exit, bold as brass. They all turned simultaneously.

'Just so you know, we know,' said Ahmed to Jamie.

'You know what?' said Jamie, a little startled.

'We know about the Cape Town Comedy Bunker,' said Ahmed. All the blood seemed to drain from Jamie's face and he visibly shuddered. He looked like he'd just seen a ghost.

'What are you going to do about it?' he asked quietly.

'Nothing we can do,' said Matt, shaking his head as Alex finished her set. 'Your dad made sure of that.'

Alex joined them and handed Matt the mic. Matt gave Jamie a disappointed look, then bounded onstage for his spot.

'How about that?' he said, pasting on a big smile. 'Alex Williams!'

Fifteen minutes later he was heading in the opposite direction, back to the wings to thunderous applause.

'Look, Matt,' said Rob, excitedly pointing to the stage. 'They're on their feet!' Matt popped his head back round the curtain – it was true. He'd got his first standing ovation!

Jamie looked at Matt ruefully.

'Go on then,' said Matt, handing him the mic. 'They're waiting for you.'

Jamie took the mic and half walked and half staggered on to the tiny stage.

'Er . . . hi!' he stuttered as he got centre stage. 'I . . . er . . .' Then he stopped and looked at Matt and the others gathered in the wings.

'What's got into Jamie?' said Alex. 'He looks ill.'

Matt just looked at her and raised his eyebrows. 'If only you knew,' he thought to himself.

Jamie coughed and then half-heartedly launched into his act. 'Hey! Thanks for waiting! Great to be here! Hey, who's got a cat here?'

Then it happened.

'Heard it,' came a voice from the back that Matt immediately recognised as belonging to Ian. The audience gasped.

'Er . . .' spluttered Jamie, unable to react to the heckle.

'Heard it,' came Ian's voice again. This time there were a few 'tuts' from the crowd, then a woman three rows from the front turned round to where she thought the heckle had come from and heckled him back. 'Shhh!' she said. 'Give the boy a chance.'

'No, no, that man, that heckler, he's right,' said Jamie quietly.

'Blimey,' said Ahmed, joining Matt and the others in the wings. 'He's 'fessing up!'

'Ladies and gentlemen, I've got a confession to make,' Jamie continued.

Then another voice joined in. 'Don't do it, son!' It was Jamie's dad.

For the first time in his young life, Jamie ignored his father's voice and pressed on. 'These aren't my jokes,' he said reaching into the pocket of his jacket and waving the printed sheets that contained his act. 'I stole them from some very funny comedians in my home country of South Africa.'

There was a gasp from the crowd.

'You idiot!' said Jamie's dad, shaking his head furiously.

'All I can say is I'd like to apologise to you and to Matt, Neil and Alex ... Ahmed and Kitty – yes, especially to Kitty,' Jamie said, choking back a tear. 'I've really enjoyed these last two weeks, it's been thrilling doing this onstage ...'

The atmosphere in the room suddenly changed from the raucous laughter during Matt's act to absolute silence – you could literally hear a pin drop. There was no stopping Jamie now. Having started his confession, the words just tumbled out, as if he'd been longing to come clean for weeks.

'If you've never tried it – stand-up comedy – it's a real buzz getting laughs. I can understand why Matt is so passionate about it, and Alex . . . I wish I was able to write jokes like them, jokes of my own, but I can't. I'm not a real comedian. I'm just pretending. I was acting being a comedian. It was just another script. I'm a fraud and I'm pulling out of the show.'

With that he hung the mic on the stand, let the printed sheets fall from his hand and, with his head low, he walked off the front of the stage, through the crowd and through the door at the back of the container. There was a stunned silence, then somebody started to clap, then another, then the whole crowd joined in.

Matt and the others looked at each other open-mouthed.

'Yup, that does it for me,' said Ahmed, nodding.

'That was really brave,' said Rob.

'What do we do now?' said Matt.

'You'd better get back out there and wind things

up,' said a voice from behind them. They looked round to see Kitty Hope, with tears in her eyes – she'd been crying.

Matt took a deep breath and walked back out on to the stage.

'So, folks, a slightly shorter show than we planned,' he said to a few pockets of awkward laughter.

43
A New King for Scotland

'I think we should go and find him,' said Matt once the audience had filed out.

They caught up with Jamie sitting on a swing in the play area round the back of Splashes, and he too had been crying. He looked at the ground and spoke slowly at first, then gathered pace.

'It was my dad's idea,' he said. 'I told him it was wrong but he's always pressurising me to come first – anything less just isn't good enough.'

'It couldn't have just been your dad,' said Ahmed. 'I mean, if my dad asked me to do something that I knew was wrong—'

'You're right, Ahmed. I saw the attention you were getting, Matt, for being so funny, and I wanted some of it.'

'"Jealousy, the green-eyed monster which doth mock the meat it feeds on,"' muttered Neil, taking a step closer.

'Eh?' said Ahmed.

'*Othello*, Act Three, Scene Three,' said Neil.

'It started off as a little thing,' continued Jamie, hitting his stride now, as if he was relieved to get the whole thing off his chest. 'You know, fifteen minutes in a school show on the edge of town – what harm could it do? Then it got out of control, ran away with me. Once people started going for it. Then that review came out and what could I do? My dad was so proud of me. It just escalated. I really loved the feeling, the laughs. I justified it by saying to myself that I was playing the part of a comedian, that I was doing a script if you like . . .'

'Look,' said Matt, stepping forward. 'You did the right thing, owning up.'

'Yeah,' said Rob. 'You put it right.'

'I can't say I'm not disappointed,' said Kitty

joining them. 'But I do understand why you did it.'

'Can you forgive me?' Jamie said in a whisper, his head bowed.

'Just this once,' said Matt. 'Oh, and it certainly proves one thing.'

'What's that?' sniffed Jamie, looking up.

'You're a really good actor!' laughed Matt, and even Jamie managed a chuckle.

As they all walked back towards the metal container to help pack the show away for the last time, they heard raised voices. Matt looked across towards the main building and saw his stepdad Ian and Ted Castle, and it was clear from their body language that they weren't catching up on old times.

'I thought I told you to keep your mouth shut?' shouted Ted, jabbing his finger into Ian's chest. 'But you couldn't help yourself, could you?'

'I know what you said, Ted,' said Ian, backing away with his hands up, trying to calm his boss. 'But it just wasn't fair on the others.'

'This wasn't about your so-called British sense

of "fair play", was it?' continued Ted, his face red, spit gathering in the corners of his mouth. 'You just couldn't bear to see my boy doing better than yours!'

The audience, which moments earlier had been sitting watching a stand-up show, were now gathering around the two men as a very different type of show unfolded.

'This is not the curtain call we expected . . .' said Matt, joining the throng.

'You're right, Ted,' said Ian, nodding. 'You're right. Britain doesn't have an empire any more, and while we're here I'm really sorry for some of the things that empire did all those years ago. But in a way we still have a sort of empire, an empire of creative thought, because we're still a nation of ideas! Yeah! It's an empire that started all those years ago with old Bill Shakespeare there,' he said, indicating a poster advertising the school's version of *Othello*. 'Don't get me wrong, I don't really get Shakespeare, but there are lot of people who do and you've got to admit, it's stood the test of time.

'Then we produced great thinkers like Isaac Newton, Stephen Hawking. Great leaders like Winston Churchill, Emmeline Pankhurst. Painters like Francis Bacon, David Hockney, Tracy Emin. Great writers like Ian Flemming, Roald Dahl and JK Rowling – and that's before you even get to the great music this tiny little island has produced. The Beatles, David Bowie . . . I happen to be a punk man myself. Yeah, 1977 and all that – The Sex Pistols, The Clash, and my personal favourite Sham 69 . . . well, one of them happened to go to school with my cousin, so maybe I'm biased. Back then, when we sang "God Save the Queen", it wasn't about empire it was about originality. About being an individual. So you can say what you like about us Brits but we don't nick other people's gear!'

There was a cheer from the crowd.

'Too right!' came a shout.

'Pah!' said Ted Castle.

'Not at all,' said Ian, calmly backing away.

'Leave it, Dad. He's right. I shouldn't have done

it!' said Jamie, bursting through the crowd to join his dad.

'You can shut up too,' snarled Ted. 'Wait till I get you home!'

'Excuse me!' came a voice from the back of the crowd. 'Excuse me!' The voice got closer to the two men until into the centre of the throng of people stumbled the slight figure of Geraint Brydon.

'Um ... may I just say something to you, Mr Castle?' said the old dancer.

'Mind your own business, old man,' growled Ted Castle.

'Well ...' Geraint hesitated then seemed to steel himself for what he was about to say next. 'Actually, it *is* my business.' Both Ian and Ted turned to face him.

'Well?' said Ted threateningly. 'I'm all ears.'

'It *is* my business and the business of anyone in this country who cares about the arts,' said Geraint, pushing his shoulders back.

'The arts, pah!' spat Ted Castle as if the words themselves contained some foul flavour.

'Yes, Mr Castle. The arts. Believe it or not, your son Jamie here has an extraordinary talent. The reason he managed to entertain all these people as a comedian for the last two weeks is because he is quite simply a brilliant actor. A talent like his is rare and should be nurtured.'

'I'll decide what's best for my son, thank you very much,' said Ted Castle, turning back to Ian.

'*No!*' said Mr Brydon sternly, warming to his theme. 'Because his talent benefits the entire community. He has a rare ability, stifle it at your peril, because if you do the world will lose a potentially great actor and you, sir, will lose a son!'

There was another round of applause from the crowd of people and Geraint tossed his hair to one side and marched dramatically back through the crowd towards the leisure centre.

Ted turned his attention back to Ian. 'I pity you, Woodwood. Stuck in a dead-end, low-paid job, because you haven't got the killer instinct you need to do well in this world!'

'Maybe I don't,' said Ian, shrugging, 'but I sleep very well at night, thank you very much.'

'Yeah? Well, you messed with the wrong family this time,' countered Ted Castle, stepping forward and jabbing Ian in the chest with his finger. 'Don't bother turning up to work on Monday because you're fired! You're fired! You hear me?'

With that he turned, grabbed Jamie by the scruff of the neck and started marching him towards their car.

'NO!' shouted Ian.

Ted stopped dead in his tracks, then slowly turned to face him. 'I'm sorry?' he said with a smirk.

'You can't sack me,' said Ian. 'Because before I came out this afternoon I delivered you a letter – it'll be waiting for you when you get back to your five-star hotel. It's a letter of resignation. You don't sack me, Ted. The spirit of Johnny Rotten lives on – I QUIT!' he shouted, punching the air with his fist. 'NO SURRENDER!'

There was a massive cheer from the crowd and a

huge round of applause as they surged forward and grabbed Ian. One bloke hoisted him up on to his shoulders and the crowd then proceeded to parade Ian around the car park, cheering him to the clear blue Edinburgh sky.

Matt looked at Rob.

'We forgot option five,' he said. 'Ian becomes the king of Edinburgh.'

44
Match Fit

It was a packed house at the Playhouse and the Anglebrook Players (minus Jamie) had great seats – Bobby had made sure of that. But as they sat waiting for the curtain to go up, Matt felt a hand on his shoulder. He looked round – it was a girl in a black T-shirt with 'CREW' written on it. 'Matt?' she said.

'Yes?' said Matt.

'I've got a message for you from Bobby,' she said and handed him a handwritten note.

HI MATT,

I'M A BIT SHORT (ACTUALLY ABOUT FIVE FOOT NINE!) OF GREAT THIRTEEN-YEAR-OLD COMICS – WOULD YOU DO FIVE MINUTES FOR ME AT THE TOP OF THE SECOND HALF?

BOBBY X

'What shall I tell him?' said the girl.

Matt didn't need to think twice.

'Tell him I'll be there!' said Matt.

Fortunately he was still in his stage suit, which had his set list in his inside pocket – although he didn't really need it. Thirteen gigs on the trot meant he was absolutely match fit.

As he stood in the wings watching Bobby getting ready to bring him on, he heard a familiar voice.

'Have a great gig!' Matt turned round to see John Beans, the young comic from The Comedy Patch. Matt smiled, nodded and shook his hand, then turned back to face the stage.

'Ladies and gentlemen, please welcome a very funny young comic and a very good friend of mine ...' Bobby looked across at Matt, and Matt suddenly felt a lump in his throat. He felt proud of his friendship with the old comic. Then he looked again at John Beans and all the other comics gathered in the wings to watch his act, and he knew in his heart that he belonged amongst them.

The two weeks of back-to-back gigs had given him a glimpse of what it could be like to be a working comic – the ups, the downs, the thrills, the disappointments, the rivalries and the camaraderie of a shared interest in making people laugh.

'It's the one and only ... Matt Millz!' bellowed Bobby.

And Matt took the stage.

That's all from him. Goodnight!

Have you read all of Matt's adventures?

Matt **LOVES** stand-up. He's studied the best, and
spends hours writing new gags . . . So when
his school runs a talent contest, of course he's
going to enter.

Then schoolmate Kitty Hope offers to coach him,
and his routine really starts to shine. Matt dares
to believe his dream of hitting the big time could
become reality. As one gig follows another,
it's not long before he's prepping for the
biggest gig of all . . .

'Probably the definitive book about being a
stand-up comedian.' **Jack Dee**

'Really funny.' **Jo Brand**

'Feel-good fiction at its best.' **BookTrust**